Other book by T.J. Mindancer

Zen
Traveler's
Heart

Zen Traveler's Heart

T.J. Mindancer

NuAnce
Books
Fairfield, California

978-1-960373-50-2 paperback

Cover Design
by

Nuance Books
a division of
Bedazzled Ink Publishing, LLC
Fairfield, California
http://www.bedazzledink.com

Dedicated to the travelers on YouTube who have kept me entertained for years.

1
Getting Ready

Zen

ZEN TROTTED ON the rocky path across the expansive high mountain meadow, the white-capped Alps rising to a glorious, cloudless sky. Spring was peeking through, and the greens were light and fresh with patches of wildflowers— bursts of yellows, whites, and blues. The cool air mixed with the sun's warmth felt great after emerging from a colder than usual winter. Her fault, so she couldn't complain about it. She went from south to north instead of from north to south to walk the longest continuous walk in the world, beginning at the tip of South Africa and reaching the northern and eastern most point of Siberia in November no less.

Her social media followers didn't deny her need to take a few weeks off, which she spent with her sister Karma in Urbana, Illinois, which of course had a cold, snowy winter.

Karma was the only person who understood how much walking the longest walk in the world had depleted her. Not so much physically. She seemed to have a physiology fine-tuned to walking, and she rarely got injured, though she did have a bit of a sensitive stomach and had been clobbered a couple of times by viruses since she had started walking full time. On the world's longest walk, she had found the outermost limits to her love of solitude several times over as she strode through endless empty lands.

She could thank Karma's brilliant editing to make walking fourteen thousand miles through sixteen countries and every possible climate and temperature extreme and political ideology and culture for a continuous twenty months sound like a fun and exciting adventure.

She shook her head. No more thinking about the past. At that moment, she was unencumbered by her usual heavy backpack and assortment of cameras, allowing her to revel in the rare chance to run, walk, and jog on a path that wound through pine groves, rugged cliff edges, and heart-stopping views of the snowy Alps around her. She broke through a line of trees and stopped to stare at the shallow valley before her. A picture-perfect Alpine village clustered around a sprawling hilltop villa filled the valley where a meandering river made a sharp bend.

She took the one camera she had with her, put it on its tripod, and positioned it to face her with the valley behind her. Using a live-view remote, she framed herself in the picture, composed what she wanted to say, and pushed record.

"First off, I want to thank all of you for taking this journey with me for the last seven years." *Pretty lame.* She stopped recording. "Just say what you want to say."

She took a settling breath and pushed record. "We've spent the last seven years together walking around this amazing planet. Now, I'm embarking on a different kind of journey."

She paused the camera as a train rumbled through the valley.

She faced the lens as the last echo of the train faded and pushed record on the remote. "Not far from here is a tiny country called Marquardt. Never heard of it? Not many people have. It closed its borders fifty-five years ago in 1969 and was under a dictator until about a year and a half ago, when the dictator died. The country decided it wanted to join the twenty-first century and elected a president to make the transition. Being in the Alps, they especially want people to visit their picturesque country. The president decided to have a test of its tourist-readiness by inviting eight solo travelers to be the first to experience Marquardt and show all of you this new place to add to your next trip to this part of the world."

She paused. Now that she had made the decision to do this trip, she wasn't quite sure how she felt about breaking the primary tenet she had made to herself as a solo traveler.

"I don't know what to expect, but I'm pretty sure I'll be with the other travelers a lot and most likely using modes of transportation other than my feet. I hope to get the opportunity to do some proper walking because from what I know about the area in general, it's gorgeous country and no doubt has many walkable trails. I hope you join me on what I'm sure will be an interesting and entertaining adventure."

She switched off the camera, turned around, and gazed at the valley. She'd never felt apprehensive at the beginning of an adventure, even when she should have, like when she embarked on the longest walk in the world. But sparks of uncertainty flitted around the edges of going to Marquardt.

The distant whoosh-whoosh of a helicopter echoed up the valley. Zen shaded her eyes against the sunlight flashing off the blades so she could see the 'copter's colors. Burgundy and white.

Zen sighed. This little adventure was turning out to be more trouble than it was probably worth. Only one thing or more specifically one person would make this trip worth everything . . . . She gave her head a shake. She could only hope this person was among the invited travelers. Hope. Such an understatement. She would give anything for the opportunity to meet her and be able to get to know her.

"I'd better get down there and see what Aunt Fiona wants." She picked up her camera and packed it away in her backpack. She ran the trail all the way to the valley floor, wanting to feel enough freedom to last a week of what will be a restrictive, but hopefully interesting adventure.

Bri

BRI ADJUSTED HER crossed legs as she settled on the oval rustic rug they had purchased from a village up the road. Thank god it fit the flat stone. She really didn't like sitting directly on stone that all kinds of critters, not to mention humans, had been on.

She pulled in a deep breath, put on a friendly tranquil face, and gazed at the camera on a tripod at the other side of a transparent pool. Josh angled the camera so it also captured the splashing waterfalls dropping down through thick foliage. Bri appreciated the effort to set up a shot that contained both her and the reason she was there. Josh could take as much B-roll as he wanted, but she was there for that one perfect shot.

Josh lifted his finger, rechecked the LED window on the camera, and pointed at Bri.

Bri took a couple of leisurely breaths as she looked around at the water, the plants, the waterfalls.

"Sometimes . . ." She gazed at the pond and raised her eyes to the camera. "Sometimes you just have to get out into nature . . . away from the city . . . away from people . . . just take in the sounds, the scents . . . the essence of being outside, away from civilization." She emitted a soft chuckle as if she was letting the viewer in on a little secret. "Of course, it doesn't hurt when the spot is as beautiful as this one."

She spent a few more minutes looking around, breathing deeply, closing her eyes as if concentrating on the sounds.

She opened her eyes. "Okay, that's enough. Get me off this rock."

Bri twisted around as Sarah scrambled through the vegetation and small boulders to get to her.

Early in her vlogging career, Bri had happily gone from city to city for her travel vlogs. Then more and more followers asked if she'd go outside the cities sometimes. Vloggers knew to pay attention to these kinds of innocent-sounding requests. If more nature meant growing viewership and keeping the followers she had, she'd try the nature thing. Unfortunately, it worked too well, and now she had to challenge Josh and Sarah to find a unique scenic place that required the least amount of communing with nature as possible. She didn't dislike nature. She just preferred to enjoy it from a car or through a train window.

Bri scooted around to face Sarah and put her hands on her shoulders as she pulled herself off the rock. "They should at least keep the path to this rock cleared."

Sarah exchanged a look with Josh, who was packing up the camera gear. Bri shook her head. *They think I'm nuts.* But really, they should make it easier to get to the flat rock because it seemed to be a favorite with visitors.

"Kind of defeats the purpose of being unspoiled by humans," Sarah muttered as she rolled up the rug.

"I heard that," Bri tossed over her shoulder as she walked gingerly through the aggressive vegetation to a path that someone had the good sense to keep nice and clear.

She shook out her fleece sleeveless vest over a long-sleeved t-shirt—glad she was wearing both because the day turned out to be cool, even for Sweden in May. Of course, the vest was a popular piece of merch displaying her logo—a tweed fedora hat with the words, Soloing With Bri—neatly embroidered on it, and she was introducing the long-sleeved shirt in a limited-time sale with the release of this vlog. The shirt ought to sell well since many followers had requested it.

She arched her neck around as she tried to look at her back. "Make sure there aren't any bugs on me."

Sarah tucked the rolled rug under her arm and checked Bri over. "You're fine, Bri."

Josh shouldered the bag of camera gear and started the very short, very flat walk to the parking lot. Bri insisted that any nature place they picked must be five-to-ten minutes from the car and required the least effort to get there. With creative framing of a shot, any outdoor place could seem as if it was way out in the middle of nowhere, so there wasn't any point in actually going out in the middle of nowhere for the same effect.

Besides, her followers didn't seem to miss the treks to and from those out of the way places other vloggers showed in detail—way too much detail, if anyone ever bothered to ask her about it. The destination was always the reason for the journey.

Bri climbed into the back of the rented SUV. Her relief as she sank into the seat felt greater than usual. This was the end of the Sweden series. It also meant being closer to an obligation she really regretted agreeing to but couldn't back out of now. Her followers had been buzzing about it since she made the announcement four weeks ago, and the last thing she wanted was to lose their interest to a fellow solo traveler. Especially if Zen Traveler had also received an invitation to participate in this unique adventure.

The vehicle rocked as Sarah climbed into the driver seat and Josh in on the passenger side.

Bri checked her watch. Three o'clock. Forty-five minutes back to the hotel in Stockholm. "Did you find the best burger place in town?"

"Barrels Burgers and Beers. It's about two blocks from the hotel," Sarah said as she maneuvered the SUV out of the gravel parking lot.

"Excellent. I've decided I'm not a big fan of Swedish food." Bri searched Barrels on her phone. It had a top rating from diners. Good.

Too bad she couldn't include eating there in her vlog, but she had established from the beginning to only showcase local food. Her vlogs were about total immersion in the local experience. That was what set her apart from the other traveling vloggers. She'd never compromised her mantra . . . on camera. But, of course, none of their on-camera personas were their off-camera lives. All of that was just a part of the game. And she knew she wasn't the only one who had a crew along on her "solo" travels. The other solo travelers couldn't possibly record the quality of videos they posted without someone else behind the camera. She was looking forward to seeing which of her fellow solo travelers struggled with capturing their footage on this invitation-only adventure.

Bri already had an excuse for the anticipated drop in the quality of her own videos. She'd say she wasn't used to scrambling for the same shot that seven other travelers were trying to shoot, and she had to change her style to adapt to this unique situation. Out of all of them, she had the most to lose because she had the most subscribers . . . excluding Zen Traveler, of course.

Zen

ZEN NODDED TO the trainee restaurant host as she strode into the dining room of the newest Benbrook property, Villa Flussbiegung. Her family had done a great job of renovating a dark, high-ceiling chamber into a light and airy space with the addition of pale beige paint and new windows overlooking a garden. The result was delicate and elegant, just the kind of place for guests who wanted to stay in five-star accommodations before and after their day-visit to the latest trendy place to visit—the country of Marquardt. At least, that's what her family was betting on.

At half-past four, tea was being served to a dining room full of people from the village who were taking advantage of a popular Benbrook tradition of offering free meals to the locals to help the kitchen and front of house staff practice their jobs and be ready when the property was opened to paying guests.

Zen spotted her aunt at a small table near the window. Zen walked around the delicate Louis XIV inspired chairs and tables made of a light-colored wood covered with white, almost wispy tablecloths. The locals were laughing and chatting as if tea at the villa was an everyday thing.

Aunt Fiona, relaxed and casual, was pouring tea into a cup as Zen slipped into the seat across from her. The amber tea whirled together with the milk at the bottom of the cup. Fiona pushed the cup on the saucer to Zen, who added a teaspoon of sugar and stirred.

Fiona held her hand out to a delicate stand of finger sandwiches and pastries. "Eat. You still look too thin from your last adventure."

"Thank you, Auntie." Zen put two cucumber sandwiches and a pastry onto her plate.

"Do you have everything you need for tomorrow?" Fiona asked.

Zen nodded. "Thanks for allowing me to store stuff here."

"I'm leaving the premier suite open for you after your trip." Fiona selected a petit four from the stand. "I have the feeling you're going to need it to decompress. This isn't going to be your usual walk in the park." Her eyes crinkled with mirth as she nibbled the small cake.

Zen rolled her eyes as she chewed a bite of the cucumber sandwich. "Am I going to have to endure walking jokes now?"

Fiona waggled her head. "Only until something better comes along." She rested affectionate eyes on Zen. "I both envy and don't envy you. I hope it's not going to be as shocking as everything indicates it's going to be, but I would really love to see it myself."

"You could go in my place," Zen said. "My clothes, a haircut, a bunch of cameras. No one will know the difference."

"Except the twenty years difference and a few inches in height." Fiona gazed out the window. "If the opportunity presents itself . . ."

"I will." As much as Zen kept away from the business side of the family business, she couldn't deny Fiona this one simple request.

2

Day 1 — Getting There

Bri

BRI LET OUT a long breath of relief as the poor excuse for a train finally stuttered to a stop. The sleek and modern express train that ran through the beautiful Alpine valley didn't stop where she was going. Unfortunately, the local train she was on stopped at or slowed way down at every place that hinted at being a village. She couldn't bring herself to shoot any footage of the long-faded interior. This was not what her viewers wanted to see from her. Between the unnerving rattle and whatever was on the tracks that was causing all the bumping and lurching, she didn't care if the station they were stopping at was her destination or not. She was getting off. Now.

A few others in the first-class car—she couldn't even imagine what a regular car looked like—were calmly collecting their belongings and leisurely poking their way to the front of the car. She glanced behind her. No one. She slipped on her backpack, pulled out the handle on her case, and strode with purpose to the rear of the car.

Bri paused at the top of the steps as the conductor who looked as ancient as the train car said something in German. He reached for the handle on her case, and she gladly let him lift it down the stairs and put it on the worn concrete platform.

"Thank you," Bri said as she stepped down to the ground.

He tipped his hat and looked to the passenger behind her.

Bri shuffled to the side and pushed her fedora back off her forehead. A one-story sooty-red brick building stood just feet away. The windows were shuttered, and the single door was propped open. She squinted down the track where a few people were climbing off the other three cars. Most of the people on the train seemed to have the good sense to keep going to another destination.

Wait a minute . . . she spotted the unmistakable signs of seasoned travelers—the backpacks and small hard-shelled suitcases, the distinctive clothes . . . the cameras . . . everyone chattering at their cameras held in front of them on sticks.

She smirked. They must have had a great time in the regular cars.

Bri strode to the depot door, her case bumping on the pitted and cracked concrete. A bus was supposed to pick them up, and she definitely wanted to get the best seat. She crossed the threshold into a dim building that could double as a barn. Her eyes watered in the smokey haze—who even smoked anymore?—and she walked past the ticket counter and a pair of rickety wooden benches. The ticket woman looked as if she hadn't smiled in years.

Bri stopped in the front doorway—her brain clearly needing time to catch up. The locals who had disembarked were climbing into waiting cars and making quick exits down the hill the village seemed to be perched on. She took several steps onto the gravel in front of the station and stared at the handful of rundown dingy buildings clinging to the edge of the randomly paved road. A very pot-holed randomly paved road. Not a road she'd call bus-worthy. This was not the charming village she liked to feature in her vlogs. Calling it a village was even a stretch.

"Whoa. This keeps getting more and more interesting."

Bri turned around. Making Tracks With Mick. No surprise there. He was one of the original solo vloggers with over a million subscribers. His GoPro was attached to his tie-dyed baseball cap with his long straight ponytail hanging out of the hole in the back of the cap. He was basically an aging hippie, born a generation after the hippie movement, from a rich Connecticut family, which he greatly played down. His Brown University degree gave him an articulate and amiable personality and a curious mind without being too intellectual. His well lived-in Levi's and cowboy shirts were as much a trademark as his baseball cap. He had a camera on a selfie-stick aimed at his face as he walked out of the depot.

He stopped walking and pointed the camera at the street for B-roll footage of the buildings.

Three others clambered through the doorway and joined him in their shooting.

Bri realized she should have her camera out to capture all this. She had no idea what to say to the camera. Sarah always knew where they were and coached her on the facts and stuff. And she forgot about the B-roll. Josh seemed to know exactly what to film and even when to film it. This place? Nothing looked interesting enough to waste a memory card on.

Bri opened her camera bag and pulled out what Josh called the main camera—at least he had charged the battery and put in the memory card. She just had to put it on the tripod stick.

"Hey, they're here!" Mick called from in front of what could be a shop of some kind . . . if it was open.

Bri looked up the road at three more vloggers, chattering to their cameras or pointing them at the buildings, trekking from around a bend in the road. That was seven so far. Where was number eight?

Bri screwed the camera onto the stick and held it out in front of her. She stared at the glassy abyss of the lens and tried to find words, any words, to say before she hit record. Panic rose up as she glanced around at her peers. They didn't seem to have any problems finding things to say, not to mention being cheerful and excited about it. They also didn't look as if they didn't know what they were doing. She pushed down her rising dread. What if she was wrong about most solo travelers having a hidden camera crew?

Wait. This was a voice-over moment. Right. The introduction where the B-footage set the tone of the video. She could come up with something to say later. She aimed the camera at the road and the buildings. The others were piling their gear in a small courtyard across the way, so she pulled her suitcase over the bumpy asphalt and added it to the motley collection of luggage.

Bri took more footage of the road, the buildings, the three goats with clanging bells on collars meandering around. It didn't look too bad in the camera window. In fact, that bit looked pretty good. *Yeah. I think I can do this.*

"A bus is coming." Flower Child—real name Kristy—trotted to the courtyard. She was an Aussie in her late twenties with flowing blonde hair held down by a black felt floppy hat with a flower ribbon. Keeping with her moniker, she wore a baggy flowery t-shirt over equally baggy cargo shorts, and clunky hiking boots. Her hook was Kind and Gentle Travel. Last time Bri checked, Kristy had 952,000 subscribers.

The others meandered down the road to the courtyard.

"I guess it's too late for second thoughts," a man with laughing eyes and a white beard said to Bri. Inquisitive George, in his seventies, was by far the oldest solo vlogger traveler. He wore khakis from head to toe as if he was always on Safari. He had some 200,000 subscribers, but he'd only been at it for three years after he handed his bookstore over to his daughters and decided to create his own stories through travel.

"I think I'm working on my fourth thoughts," Bri said. She actually liked George. He had a nice little vlog.

Jon of All Trades bounced up to them. He was from Norway and was one of those enthusiastic young men who still had idealistic thoughts about saving the world through extolling the greatness of its wonders and diverse cultures. He had quickly built his subscriber base to 750,000 with his China series. He could be a threat in the race for subscribers in the near future if he kept up the momentum and his over-abundance of youthful enthusiasm didn't overstay its visit.

"Nothing to think about." He almost vibrated in his excitement. "We're going to be a part of history. How cool is that?"

"Very minor history." Adventure Girl—Sally in real life—in her Adventure Girl T-shirt, and her trademark olive drab pants and Chucks, picked up her backpack. She pushed back the mop of black hair from her forehead and shaded her eyes as she watched the progress of the bus. She had 350,000 subscribers. Not bad for a part timer.

The bus, painted a stunningly ugly blue, whined and screeched its way past the buildings.

"I think I rode one of those when I was a kid," George said.

"Definitely not of this century or even a good part of last century." Joe the Historian stood with his hands on his hip as he watched the questionable progress of the bus. He had only 162,000 subscribers, but that was pretty good for history-heavy content. He sacrificed comfort and practicality for a heather blue wool suit that had lost its shape dozens of countries ago and scuffed patches on the elbow for the academic look. At least he wore a practical shirt with no tie.

Kristy lifted her camera to get a better shot of the bus. "No one mentioned time travel."

"Isn't that right up your alley?" Jon of All Trades jumped away from her playful swipe at him.

Bri wondered who the missing eighth traveler was and what would happen if they missed the bus.

Zen

WITH THE GOPRO recording from the backpack strap below her shoulder, Zen walked across the stone bridge that acted as the southern boundary to the village and exhaled as she always did when the combined feeling of freedom and starting a new adventure washed over her. Sure, the walking part of this adventure ended after only seven miles, but it was still something new. New was always the operative word for her travels, even if no one was aware of that little detail.

She walked a bit down the two-lane paved road, then stopped recording. She took her primary camera, already on the tripod from her bag, set it up alongside the road, and walked away from it. After a few minutes, she ran back to retrieve it. As she strode down the road, she continued the routine of recording with several cameras, different angles, coming and going . . .

She came to a road that looked as if it hadn't been maintained for years. She studied the road as it wound upward out of the valley and disappeared into a thick stand of trees. The road had one small village with a train station a few miles from where she stood and then continued on for several more miles until it ended at the Marquardt border.

This was the point of no return. She looked back. The villa sat on its little hill like an impressionistic painting of yellows and whites. She went to the opposite side of the paved road and placed her camera so it captured her turning onto the unpaved road. Unlike her usual journeys where her schedule was her own, she had to be at the little village by a certain time and to maintain a faster pace than she liked to take.

She walked up the hill with a canopy of trees turning the road into a dark meandering trek. She heard a train enter the valley from the direction of the villa and knew that was how the other travelers would most likely be arriving at the village. She pulled out her drone, launched it, and guided it up the hill until the village appeared maybe a mile as the bird flew from where she stood. She recorded the village from different angles. As the train pulled into the tiny station, Zen positioned the drone to have a good view of the people exiting the train. Yep. Several vloggers clambered out . . .

Her breath caught as she moved the drone closer to a car in the front. Bri—as in Soloing With Bri—stepped off the train. Zen concentrated on holding the drone steady as her mind flew through so many emotions she felt lightheaded. Bri disappeared into the train station, and Zen pulled the drone away and guided it back to her.

She couldn't resist looking at the footage before packing the drone away.

"She's here. She's really here."

Her one wish for the week. A wish that would make the week worthwhile. And now . . . She gazed at the footage again. And now . . . *Oh my god* . . . How would she ever survive?

Bri

BRI LOOKED DOWN the road away from the village, hoping that was the direction they were heading. Someone was striding up the hill. Earth-colored T-shirt under a light jacket, practical state-of-the-art hiking pants, backpack . . .

"Well, well." Mick shaded his eyes. "Looks like your archrival got an invitation."

Zen Traveler. Four-point-five-million subscribers. One million, two hundred thousand more subscribers than Bri's vlog channel.

"Hardly a rival," Bri said, putting on a pleasant good-sport smile. "She had an amazing series when she trekked the longest walk in the world. You know how it is."

"Tell me about it," Mick said. "You never know what viewers are going to jump all over."

George nodded. "If we knew, we'd all be making *those* videos."

They watched as Zen set up her camera along the road, shot herself walking past it, and then trotted back to pick up the camera. She continued walking, aiming the camera ahead of her as she strode into the village.

Fit was the first word anyone would think when seeing Zen. Her body was muscular but lean and quite androgynous, which came in handy when she traveled through places considered dangerous for women. That was especially true during her longest walk series. She kept her black hair close-cropped, most likely to control the tousle of curls spilling onto her forehead.

Bri had to admit, she was conflicted about her. If there was such a thing as a rivalry in their business, Zen would be Bri's greatest adversary. But how could one set eyes on this calm woman who patiently tread the world, finding the best in people everywhere, and think of her as a rival?

Zen aimed her camera at the bus as she walked past it and did a tour of the town, shooting the buildings with a quiet efficiency that set the tone of all her vlogs.

"Morning, Zen." Joe gave Zen a jaunty salute.

"Beautiful morning," Zen said.

She flashed Bri a shy grin and trailed along behind the group as they trudged to the bus on a cleared patch next to the road on the edge of town. Bri glanced back at Zen who wasn't even breathing hard after probably walking for miles through the mountainous countryside. Must be nice to be that fit.

The door of the bus stuttered then jerked open. They all stepped back in surprise. A thin man, maybe in his forties, with slicked-back blond hair and dressed in a white polo shirt and dark slacks that looked like something George's father would have worn, climbed down the steps and clasped his hands with an excited grin. He was like a character out of a Fellini movie, if Fellini had been German.

"Travelers," he carefully enunciated in a thick German accent. "I'm so glad to see you all." He looked them over as if he was counting. He then frowned and studied each of them as if confirming who they were. "Yes. You've all made it." His voice had an odd, puzzled tone. "Thank you. Thank you. Excuse me a minute." He stepped back into the bus, pulled the stuttering door closed, and carried on a rather animated conversation presumably on his phone, ending with what sounded like a reluctant agreement to something.

Zen, wearing a puzzled expression, cocked her ear to the door.

Bri exchanged uncertain looks with the others. What *had* they gotten themselves into?

The door creaked open, and the man emerged at the top of the steps. "Thank you for your patience. Please, please. Climb aboard. I'm Viktor, your assistant and guide."

Bri definitely wanted to be the first one on board to assess the degree of awfulness and get first dibs on the best place to sit. She stepped forward.

"Oh, allow me." Victor scurried down the steps, grabbed her case, and pulled it into the bus.

"Thank you?" Bri sputtered. She walked up the steps and was pleased to see a surprisingly clean, but very basic bus from probably the 1960s. Kind of like the ancient city buses from her childhood.

She took possession of the first-row seat that was not behind the driver and put her case next to the aisle. Not that she thought anyone else was going to want to share a seat. She dropped her backpack onto the aisle seat and settled in next to the window.

Viktor scrambled back down the steps and reappeared with Sally's case. Sally stomped up the steps, looking none too happy.

"Thanks, but I can handle my own stuff," she muttered as she grabbed the handle of the case and dragged it down the aisle.

Viktor stared after her with a profoundly puzzled expression as Mick and John filed past him. He looked out the door, gasped, and scrambled down the steps. "Let me, let me."

He reappeared with Kristy's case, and she glared at him as she yanked the handle from him. He stared at her back, looking so confused.

George and Joe scooted past Viktor as he got ready to run down the steps again. Bri looked behind her to see Sally and Kristy stopping in mid-settling in to watch the door. Zen walked up the steps as calm and unbothered as usual as Viktor hurried up after her, looking as if he was ready to burst something important.

Of course, Zen didn't have a case for Viktor to grab. She traveled with a two-tier backpack that was no doubt custom-made to fit all her stuff efficiently with the lightest weight. Bri watched Zen make her way to the back of the bus, marveling at the powerful set of shoulders and back muscles that allowed her to walk around all day as if forty or fifty pounds were nothing.

The noise level rose as everyone talked to or aimed their cameras around the interior. At least the bus was big enough so they could take up two seats, even a whole row.

Viktor seemed to have recovered his cheerful mood as he grinned and clasped his hands, waiting until everyone was settled.

"This is the part where the audience, 'yells get off the bus,'" Joe the Historian muttered from his seat directly behind Bri.

She had to admit she was thinking the same thing. She looked over the back of her seat and realized he was talking to his camera. So much for giving positive first impressions to his viewers. Everyone else continued to shoot Viktor, the bus, or themselves.

Showing footage of the travel between destinations wasn't a part of Bri's vlogs. She seriously thought most travelers went overboard including all the details of the actual travel. How many times did a viewer need to see someone getting on and off a plane, or roaming through an airport, or riding Ubers across town? It felt as if they were padding their vlogs with pointless content.

Bri looked around the bus and up at Viktor. It was true, this wasn't just another bus to anywhere. This was the beginning of an adventure to a place no one had been to in fifty-seven years. Her camera was peeking out from a side pocket in the backpack. Sighing, she pulled it out and focused it on Viktor and then stood and did a long shot of the rest of the bus.

"If everyone is settled, it's time to get going," Viktor said, obviously not used to a group of travelers focused solely on getting good footage.

Mick, seated opposite Bri in the next row back, looked around and blasted a whistle through his fingers. Everyone turned to him, startled. Viktor stared at him with wide, frightened eyes.

"The man wants to get this show on the road." Mick nodded at Viktor.

Everyone muttered apologies, sat down, and aimed their cameras at Viktor.

Viktor blinked at them, as if realizing he was going to be a part of the vlogging experience. He fluttered his hands and then smoothed down his shirt. "Please be seated. We are ready to leave."

We, meaning him, since he was also the driver. Everyone sat while still talking to their cameras or aiming them around the bus.

Viktor gave them all one last look and slipped behind the oversized steering wheel. The motor sputtered to life on the fourth try. Not a promising start. He did some elaborate shifting and wiggling of the gear stick, and the bus lurched forward, rolled backward, and, after some frantic shifting, forward. He slowly eased the bus onto the road. Then backed up, went forward, backed up, went forward, until the bus was facing the town.

Bri exchanged alarmed looks with everyone else.

"Was hoping we weren't going up the hill," Joe the Historian said.

"Is the road better, at least?" Bri asked as she pointed her camera at the buildings as the bus crunched around the bend.

Joe shook his head. "Not from what I saw. Rocky, hugging the edge of the mountain . . ."

"Anyone know how far it is?" Sally asked.

"Seventeen kilometers to the border," Joe said. "The condition of the road will make it feel like a hundred."

Jon put down his camera. "In other words, Zen would beat us walking."

Everyone chuckled. Bri arched her neck to see Zen's reaction. Zen grinned and tilted her head in amusement.

The bus jumped and lurched. Viktor battled the gears some more. Walking didn't sound like such a terrible idea.

3
Day 1 — Arriving
Zen

ZEN STAKED OUT the back of the bus, as far away from Bri as possible. She didn't want to be seated where the temptation to gawk at her was too great, and she certainly wasn't ready to actually talk to her for fear of babbling nonsense.

She grabbed the seat in front of her as the bus bumped around a sharp upward curve. Was it too late to get off and just walk? She had promised herself and Fiona that she would be a part of the group. Being a part of them was the only way to understand Marquardt's tourist-readiness.

"I hope Austria improves this road," Kristy, one row in front of her, muttered.

Zen sat forward. "The road on the Italian side is very well kept and well-travelled."

Kristy and a couple of the others turned to her.

"Really?" Jon asked. "Then why are we going in this way?"

Zen shrugged. "You have to cross a bridge to get to Marquardt and it's blocked. It also doesn't have an official border entry point."

"That'll change, I'm sure." Kristy was almost flung off her seat as the bus took another curve much, much too fast. "Don't they learn to drive in Marquardt?"

Zen cocked her head. "Probably not, come to think of it. They don't have many motor vehicles and only a few paved roads."

"How are they expecting people to get around?" Sally asked.

Zen shrugged. "Guess we'll find out."

To take her mind off of Viktor's inability to control the bus, Zen put fresh batteries into her GoPro and primary camera. She studied the window. Easy enough to open. Karma would kill her if she crashed another drone. But she'd also love the footage if the drone didn't crash. Zen took her second drone with a fresh battery and memory card from her bag.

She programmed the control to follow-me mode. Now she just had to wait for the perfect moment to set it flying.

She sat back and tried to get a glimpse of Bri. *I hope I don't make a fool of myself around her.*

Bri

THE BUS ROCKED, a little too violently, onto what looked like a freshly paved and painted road after they rolled past the border with its guards in severe beige military uniforms and hulking beige buildings. Inviting in a cold war bunker kind of way. Bri hoped they had plans for a friendlier "welcome tourist" makeover.

They were in a narrow high mountain valley with just enough room for a river surrounded by lush green on one side of the road and cultivated fields on the other side before tree-covered hills and snowy mountains rose up on both sides. The houses and buildings were typical Alpine wood-framed, and like the road, looked as if they had a fresh coat of paint, the fences all precise and straight, the side of the road neatly trimmed . . . almost too pristine to be lived in. Bri wondered if the rest of the country had been cleaned up, so to speak, to make a good impression for the coming deluge of tourists.

She aimed the camera out the window, trying to hold it steady as the bus seemed to hit every bit of unevenness in the pavement at breakneck speed.

Looking outside was too scary, so Bri watched her fellow travelers as they jolted around and grumbled to each other. Zen pulled down the window and released something out of it. *What the . . . ?* She was manipulating something in her hands. Bri never took Zen to being into gadgets, but, then again, she had to have the technology to produce her amazingly beautiful footage.

The bus veered around a sharp turn that pushed Bri hard against the window as they climbed out of the valley. Viktor flew the bus up the curvy road through the dip in the mountains without understanding the nuances of using the gas pedal—like letting up every once in a while and not pressing down on it so hard.

Bri glanced back, and everyone was clutching the seat in front of them, terror in their wide eyes. Even Zen looked mildly alarmed as she jerked back and forth while still manipulating whatever was in her hands. Bri was glad she wasn't the only one frightened out of her mind. Fortunately, they hadn't encountered any other vehicles or stray animals. Maybe they had put out a red alert that Viktor was driving the bus today.

The road flattened and expanded into two lanes both ways, the paint on the lines still glistening. Bri looked ahead through the windshield and was almost blinded by a building, maybe five or six stories high, sparkling in the late afternoon sun. It morphed into an ordinary-looking downtown-type structure perched on top of a small hill. Viktor finally figured out where the brake was and slowed down enough to enter a parking lot, turn onto a concrete curved driveway, and squeak to a shuddering stop in front of what looked like a typical convention hotel.

The travelers' collective exhale of breath would have been comical, if it wasn't, well, a genuine spontaneous display of relief.

"I was praying so hard I think I just converted to some religion," Mick said as he flopped back in his seat.

Viktor, all smiles, jumped out of the driver's seat and clasped his hands together. "You are the first guests in our brand new, state-of-the-art hotel. Welcome." He jiggled the long door handle and pushed. The door stuttered and jerked open.

"Well, I'm out of here." Bri stood, shouldered her backpack, and grabbed the handle of her case. She blew past Viktor, not even giving him a chance to get his hand out. *I'm a pro at lifting my case and carrying it up and down steps, thank you very much.* She walked to about ten feet from the bus to keep out of the way.

Viktor scampered off the bus after Bri and hovered while aimlessly moving his hands around as she parked the case on the concrete. As if realizing he missed his opportunity to help, he turned to the steps and gasped as Kristy and Sally climbed down and pulled their cases next to Bri.

Viktor looked as if he was going to say something but returned his attention to the bus as everyone else clambered off—Zen between Joe and George—further thwarting his weird chauvinist behavior.

Bri looked around. The driveway and parking lot was even newer than the roads. The concrete had no marks or discoloration from vehicles. They were under a four-car-wide canopy that extended from a wall of glass with a row of glass doors standing open presumably for them. Everything was so fresh and new, from the valet stand to the welcome mats in front of the door, she could smell the drying paint.

Bri certainly hadn't expected a brand-new building that was a painstaking replica of an ordinary convention hotel. Unimaginative corporate aesthetic with enough reflective glass all around to keep the small bird population under control. Where was the local color experience?

The other vloggers clustered around Bri, looking equally befuddled.

Jon glanced at the doors. "Not what I expected."

Zen, standing on the side of the huddle away from the bus, manipulated a small control. A palm-sized drone swooped under the canopy and landed on the concrete next to her. She scooped it up, turned it off, and slipped it into her pocket.

A drone. Bri couldn't help but marvel at how Zen could fly it without fuss and very little attention. She looked at the bus. Viktor was trying to get the door to shut. Of course, Zen would wait until Viktor was distracted to bring down her drone.

"Are we anywhere near the town?" Kristy walked toward the road at the side of the building.

Viktor turned to her with widening eyes and almost tripped as he rushed after her. "Stop. What are you doing?"

Kristy gave him a puzzled look. "Just looking around."

Viktor chuckled nervously. "Yes. Solo traveler. I get it. But it's best if you wait."

"For what?"

"Yes. Humor. You're very good." Viktor waved his hands as if he was trying to shoo her back to the rest of them.

Kristy gazed at Bri and the other travelers with profound confusion as she followed Viktor.

What have we gotten ourselves into? Bri exchanged bewildered glances with the others.

"Gotta admit, that was strange," Mick said.

Viktor nervously glanced around as he tried to smile pleasantly. "Please. Go inside. You're our first guests."

Bri found herself behind Zen as they crossed the threshold into a glassy two-story lobby with lots of sparkling metal fixtures and a reflective marble floor polished to a blinding gleam. The chairs and sofas looked too soft to be comfortable with bland beigey colors woven into a vague pattern. Off-the-shelf furniture for a typical downtown hotel. Zen wore a mild appraising expression as she looked around. Her family, the Benbrooks, had dominated the hospitality industry for a century and pretty much owned the Alpine tourist trade.

"What do you think?" Bri asked.

Zen blinked at her then tilted her head a bit. "It's interesting."

Bri chuckled. She could only imagine what Zen was thinking.

"All right. Gather around." Viktor put himself in front of the marble service counter.

A pair of young men in identical blue suits, perfect ties, and slicked down hair stood at attention behind the counter.

"Okay. First thing first." He turned to Bri and Zen and then to Kristy and Sally. "I get it. For the cameras you have to look like you travel alone. We get it. We've sent a car to pick up your husbands, so you don't have to worry."

What? Bri looked at Kristy and Sally, who shared the same shocked expressions.

Sally's expression turned to outrage. "We're solo travelers."

Viktor grinned and nodded. "Of course. You put on a good show. But, of course, your husbands are with you."

Sally put her hands on her hips. "I don't have a husband. I travel alone."

"I'm certainly not married," Kristy said. "Solo. Means solo."

Bri glanced around and shrugged. "No husband." Or wife. She pictured trying to explain *that* to Viktor.

Viktor's expression was uncomprehending as he turned to Zen, who shook her head with an amused expression.

"Trust me, she's not married . . . at least to a man," Sally said.

Viktor frowned with momentary confusion and then smiled as he clasped his hands together. "Yes, yes. I get it. We promise we won't let your secret out. It's good watching. The novelty of women traveling alone."

"I don't think he believes you," George muttered.

"Why would you think we have husbands?" Kristy asked, her body stiff with indignation.

"I guess you didn't brush up on the history of this place," Joe said. "Very archaic attitude toward women."

Zen scratched her head. "I was hoping that had been dealt with during the year of learning to be progressive."

"Your husbands are okay with you pretending you're not married?" Viktor crossed his arms, plainly not believing anything they were saying.

Bri all but threw up her hands. "If there's a problem that we're unmarried, then there's a problem with us being here."

An obnoxious ringtone filled the air. Viktor pulled his old-time flip phone from his pocket and engaged in a rather spirited conversation.

"It's about not finding husbands," Zen said quietly.

Bri stared at Zen and remembered she had a knack for languages and was fluent in several of them. That, of course, came from literally growing up all over the world. She knew that Zen had been born in Greece but didn't know her true nationality, since the Benbrook clan was as International as their business. Because Zen spoke perfect English with an American accent, everyone just assumed she was from the States. Then again, it could have been from going to school in California. That language skill would certainly come in handy in this strange place.

Viktor re-pocketed his phone with a long sigh. He looked as if he was reluctantly making a decision, then turned to the service counter and gave what seemed to be very surprising and not very well-received instructions to the young men. One of them responded with what sounded like an indignant protest. Viktor leveled some stern words at them, and they took down four of the neatly lined-up packets on the counter—presumably the room cards and welcome info. They typed into their computers, the printers came to life, and they swiped room cards and repacked the packets.

Viktor returned his attention to the travelers, hands clasped, back in host mode. "No problem. As you know, it's not proper for women to stay in a hotel room alone, so two will share. Problem solved, until your husbands show up."

Bri exchanged alarmed glances with the others. Kristy opened her mouth. Zen gave her head a shake, and her calm persona seemed to make Kristy think better of whatever she was going to say.

"Sounds like a wise solution," Zen said to Viktor.

Zen

VIKTOR HANDED OUT the packets to each traveler. Kristy and Sally compared cards and grinned. Zen and Bri exchanged nods as Zen tried to calm her scattered reactions to the idea of actually sharing a room with Bri.

Viktor picked up a sheet of paper. "Let me introduce you to the amenities . . ."

Zen looked at the keycard packet. First floor. She glanced around and found the signs to the rooms a few feet away. The inanity of the situation was setting off her need to move, and Viktor was making her exponentially antsy.

Just wait for the right moment . . .

A few minutes later, Viktor turned and gestured at the front doors. Zen ghosted around the corner into an area with a closed half-filled gift shop and a couple of other small spaces probably meant for retail. Aunt Fiona would be extremely unhappy on the outside and raging mad on the inside if one of her properties was not one hundred percent ready the moment it was opened to guests. Her extremely unhappy expression was enough to have everyone trembling in fear and scurrying around to fix whatever needed fixed.

Zen stopped and looked back. It made sense for Bri to be her roommate. Kristy and Sally were younger and had more in common, so they would most likely have more fun together. She and Bri were about the same age, early forties. They even started travel vlogging at about the same time and seven years later they were still at it.

Thank goodness for that. Bri's weekly vlogs were her guilty pleasures. She had even made sure she could get Internet on Wednesdays when she had been on the longest walk. This strategic planning was often the only thing that kept her going when she felt as if she was a thousand miles away from the nearest human.

Sheesh. I've got it bad. She continued to the bank of elevators and turned onto a wing of rooms. Number 101. She'd bet anything Kristy and Sally had been assigned the opposite room.

She slipped the keycard into the slot, walked in, and stopped. The design was so basic, she could probably walk around it blindfolded and identify where everything was. She peeked into the bathroom, which was next to the door with a little closet opposite it. The quality of the fixtures, the tiles, the plastering, the wood . . . barely scraped past adequate for typical hotel use. Not surprising, considering who won the contract to build this monstrosity.

She entered the room proper—almost double the size of a regular hotel room, which she was not unhappy about. Bumping into and squeezing around Bri was something she didn't want to do until she got used to being around her.

She dropped her backpack onto the bed closest to the window. "Snap out of it. It's just a crush. A massive crush."

Yeah, and Zen would accept it as a crush and hope they could become friends if she hadn't found out one small detail Bri forgot to include in her official bio . . . Bri's own fault for going to the University of Illinois and being in the same department as Karma at the same time.

"I can casually flirt." Zen nodded as she pulled a pair of jeans and a t-shirt from her pack. "No one would think twice about that."

Sometimes having a wild, misspent youth came in handy.

Bri

BRI LET LOOSE a relieved breath as she dragged her case into her assigned room. Frazzled didn't even begin to describe how she felt. Too much confusing drama, and she didn't like drama. At all.

She stared at the room as her brain caught up. She was a little disappointed but not surprised that it was a pretty basic hotel room, just oversized. Nicely oversized. She paused at the bathroom and flipped on the light. Roomy with almost blinding silver fixtures, faux fancy everything, trying too hard to impress. At least the flush and the faucets worked.

Two beds were on one side of the room and a generous sized sitting area with twin desks and a huge wall tv on the other side. The décor was low key with blonde wood furniture. Functional, basic hotel stuff. Just like in the lobby.

Zen was standing next to the bed closest to the window, pulling her camera equipment from her backpack. Good. Bri preferred to be next to the bathroom. She lifted her backpack off her shoulders and dropped it onto the bed. Who knew it could get so heavy in such a short amount of time?

"You're now officially the envy of everyone," Bri said. "Ghosting away like that."

Zen straightened. "Viktor seems to aggregate my tolerance level for silliness."

Bri chuckled as she kicked off her shoes and sat on the bed.

Zen took her laptop to the desk opposite her bed.

"What did you think about all that husband nonsense and needing to help us with our bags?" Bri removed a fresh shirt and a pair of jeans from her case. "They spent a year learning about and adapting to modern times. How'd they miss all the women vigorously hacking away at the patriarchy for the last half century?"

"Sometimes they see only what they want to see and then fit it into their narrow world," Zen said as she put her laptop on the desk and studied the desk level power strip. "Like they think it's acceptable for us to pretend to be solo travelers because it's a fanciful entertainment for them and, of course, we're not really solo travelers and have husbands who travel with us."

Bri frowned at her as she tried to imagine anyone in the twenty-first century thinking like that. "So, they really believe we're putting on an act for the camera?"

Zen turned the desk chair to face Bri and sat down. "That's what it looks like."

Unbelievable. "Then what are we going to do about it?"

Zen shrugged. "Be ourselves. If they don't like what they're seeing, they may need to rethink opening their borders."

Bri gazed as Zen for a few moments. Zen was known for working through situations with a calm steadiness and a positive attitude, spawning some entertaining, at times heated discussions on social media. Mostly people chiming in on what they would have done if they were her. At this moment, Bri could believe that the Zen Traveler was really as Zen as she appeared in her vlogs. Truly living up to her actual birth name.

One thing for sure, she was glad she was not rooming with either Adventure Girl or Flower Girl—they were too young and excitable for her. Although she admitted she'd love to know what they were talking about at that moment.

4
Day 1 — First Night
Zen

THIS ISN'T SO bad. It actually feels kind of . . . comfortable? Like we can be friends if . . . well, friends would be good. Zen glanced at the bed where Bri was sprawled on her back, scrolling on her phone. The wifi seemed to be excellent—at least in the hotel. Who knew about the rest of the country.

Zen opened the memory card from a drone and stared at the thumbnails of the village. She glanced back at Bri again. She pulled out three videos and put them in a new folder she labeled "B."

"Wow." Bri rolled over on the bed. "Where's this?" She held her phone out and Zen squinted at the screen.

Zen's Instagram. "That's a village seven or eight miles from where we got on the bus."

"Is that where you stayed last night?"

Zen nodded. "My family bought a villa there and renovated it into a small hotel. It officially opens in a week in anticipation of a new stream of tourists interested in visiting Marquardt."

Bri pulled herself up and sat cross-legged. "I have a million questions."

Zen laughed. "I'm not sure if I have a million answers."

Bri looked around the room. "Fortunately, we have all week."

A long-dormant joy bubbled up inside Zen. She had a week to win Bri's heart.

Bri

BRI WAS STARVING. Besides traveling all day, the bag of stale chips and bottle of cola for lunch lasted about as long as it took to consume them. The restaurant could have been open when they had arrived, but the not-so-perceptive people in charge wanted to have a grand opening, beginning at six. But they promised it would be open twenty-four-seven after that. Never mind, they were all starving now. At least, Bri was.

At quarter to six Bri practically dragged Zen out of the room so they'd be there when the restaurant opened. They barely took two steps toward the lobby before they were hit by a wall of noisy chatter.

Bri looked at Zen. "What the . . . ?"

The noise increased as they passed the elevators and entered the retail area. As if reading each other's mind, they stopped before turning the corner to the lobby and exchanged apprehensive looks.

"Do you think they actually put the *grand* in grand opening?" Bri asked.

Zen let out a sigh. "I truly hope not."

"Well, if there's a crowd between me and getting dinner in a timely manner, they're going to get a nasty review on Yelp."

Zen stared at Bri as if she was crazy and sputtered a laugh.

Bri shrugged. "I'm not pleasant when I get too hungry."

"Noted," Zen said, trying to look solemn but couldn't stop an amused smile.

They stepped around the corner and stopped . . . and stared. Bri made sure her mouth wasn't hanging open—she couldn't do anything about her eyes being filled with shock.

The lobby was beyond crowded, sloshing, more like it, with boisterous very Germanic adults with refugees from the senior community liberally mixed in, all looking and acting as if they just got off the Octoberfest train straight from Munich. They chattered in exuberant German, clearly excited and proud of this glassy, shining example of Western capitalistic lack of imagination they were standing in.

Somewhere on the far side of the lobby was the restaurant entrance. It may as well have been in Siberia for Bri to get food in a timely manner, even if the special foreign visitors had their own table. The kitchen would be swamped with orders. Again, Bri realized how much she relied on Sarah and Josh to keep everything moving smoothly by making reservations and ensuring restaurants had certain foods and . . .

Zen nudged Bri and nodded to one side. Sally and Kristy were skirting the wall toward them. The locals were giving them surprised, shocked, and a few disapproving looks, sometimes all at the same time. What were they going to do when modern Western women in all their liberated glory descended on their tiny, insulated world?

Sally sidled up next to Bri and Zen and glanced around with a wry expression. "Guess what the biggest event in the country is?"

"Maybe they wanted more than eight people at the grand opening," Bri said.

"I heard the president was supposed to be here, but he's still up to his eyebrows in working out those pesky last-minute details for opening a country to the world." Kristy pressed against the wall as if it could miraculously absorb her into a parallel universe that had a crowd-free dinner. "Viktor looked as if he had been granted a reprieve from the executioner. I think he hasn't told the higher ups about us."

Several locals spotted them and shot very disapproving looks while exchanging whispered comments.

"They definitely need to work on being more welcoming," Bri said.

Kristy snorted a laugh.

"We grabbed a menu." Sally held up a laminated booklet with gaudy photos of food on the cover.

Bri frowned. "Looks like a menu from Denny's."

"Yep." Sally opened it to the first page. "Instead of giving tourists the opportunity to sample the local cuisine, they thought we would want typical Western food. Hamburgers, tacos, pizza, fries, fish and chips . . . steaks, baked potatoes . . . My arteries are clogging just holding this thing."

Bri chuckled with the others, even though she preferred a good hamburger over most local food.

"American culture was probably the only part of the modern world they heard about in the last fifty years," Zen said. "It may have been decried by the government as decadent and the downfall of civilization but the first thing people want when liberated from that kind of government control is a hamburger and to visit Disneyland. Only fitting that's what they want to embrace now."

"I asked about the vegetarian menu. The guy in charge of the restaurant proudly showed us the last page." Kristy nodded at the menu as Sally turned and presented it to Zen.

Zen took the menu and held it so Bri could see it.

"It says vegetarian at the top, but it's all meat," Zen said.

"Correction." Kristy held up a finger. "It's all chicken and fish with lots of vegetables and salads. That's how they interpreted the vegetarian diet. Meat is beef and pork and lamb to them."

Zen sighed.

"And I bet the vegetables are laced with meat juice and broth." Kristy closed the menu. "The last thing I want tonight is a salad."

Zen glanced at a close-by glass outside door. "There's a raclette restaurant a couple of blocks away."

Bri, Sally, and Kristy snapped their attention to her.

"Really?" Kristy tilted her head. "How do you know that?"

Zen shrugged. "I tapped into my family's research."

Sally gave her a speculative look. "Hmmm. You could be useful to have around."

Zen smiled. "I'll share what I can."

"But what about money?" Bri asked. "We haven't been able to convert our Euros."

"Their currency isn't worth anything, so euros will be the accepted currency here, once the border opens," Zen said.

Sally looked out over the sea of locals. "Should we tell the boys?"

"I'm not wading into that mess to look for them," Kristy said. "Besides, I don't want to run into Viktor."

"We'll slip out the side door," Zen said.

"What about the female issue? What if the restaurant refuses to serve us?" Bri gazed out at the crowd, willing Viktor to not suddenly emerge and descend on them.

Zen cocked her head with an amused expression. "The owner is a woman. They allow women to inherit certain businesses from a husband if there aren't any male offspring. Selling food is close enough to women's work so they allow it. And she was very interested in working with my family and wasn't happy when the government didn't contract with us."

Sally aimed her camera at the crowd. "Need some local color B-roll. Before we split this scene."

Bri watched her in sudden panic. How could she forget to bring a camera? And they were sneaking out to a local establishment. This kind of rebellious adventuring was exactly what she should be shooting. She turned to Zen, who was wearing what looked like a custom-made utility belt with several different sized pockets—a couple with small cameras peeking out. Of course, with all the money rolling in from her vlogs, not to mention being a member of one of the richest dynasties in the world, Zen could buy the very best gear and have it custom made.

"Here," Zen said quietly as she pulled a small camera, half the size of a phone, from her belt. "I haven't used this one, so the memory card is empty."

Bri glanced at Sally and Kristy who were focused on shooting, Sally was even talking to her camera.

Zen put the camera in Bri's hand.

"Uh, thanks." Bri studied the camera, aimed it at the crowd, and let it roll for a bit.

"Let's drift to the door," Sally said, continuing to aim her camera at different points in the lobby.

The loudspeaker crackled on and emitted what sounded like garbled German. The crowd excitement and noise crescendoed as everyone faced the restaurant side of the lobby with startling precision.

"They're getting ready to open, which means Viktor will probably be looking for us." Zen sidled to the door, opened it, and slipped out.

Sally and Kristy followed her out without hesitation. Bri glanced back, scooted out through the doorway, and pushed the door closed.

The cool evening air hit Bri, and she sucked in a relieved breath. Relieved to be both away from the suffocating lobby and to be free. The sun sat low on the horizon and illuminated a valley of surprisingly quaint alpine shops in a tight area of winding blocks split by narrow cobblestone lanes. The glistening glass monstrosity they were standing next to seemed to be on the very edge of town.

A low rumble of voices spilled around the corner from the front of the hotel, in contrast to the silent, empty-looking town.

"So, they take us to a Hyatt clone and right next to it is this," Sally was saying to her camera. She turned her camera around to take in the tourist idea of a typical Alpine village.

Kristy glanced back. "We'd better get away from the windows."

"This way." Zen led the way to the first crossroad at the back of the hotel. The quaint downtown area continued into the valley one way, but the other way up the hill had modern structures that were so new, the small attempts at landscaping looked as if they had been planted yesterday.

"Dear god," Sally murmured. "They think urban ugly is being modern?"

Kristy squinted as she studied the new buildings. "Looks like they're planning to move in some fast-food joints."

Zen sighed.

Bri gave her a sidelong look. "Why isn't your family here?"

Zen pushed her hands into the front pockets of her jeans as they walked on the deserted cobblestone lane into the town proper. "Their bid wasn't accepted."

Kristy lowered her camera and turned to Zen. "You mean they wouldn't work with a business run by a woman."

"That's the way my aunt understood it." Zen stopped in front of a door.

Bri stepped back and studied the bay window creating a niche large enough for a small table and chairs. The wooden door and window were decorated with what were probably the popular mountain motifs for the area. The name of the restaurant, Frau Mueller's, filled the window in ornate script.

Zen pulled open the heavy wood door, and they walked into a spacious establishment with a rustic, beer garden veneer. Bri stood to the side in front of the service stand as they all huddled near the door.

"Wait here," Zen mumbled and approached a thin older woman in a frilly apron, who was seated at one of the dozen or so empty tables. The woman stood so fast, she wobbled the table, and stared at them as if they were from another planet.

Zen, talking in a low friendly voice, put out her hand. The woman blinked at it and shook it. She then frowned and looked down into her hand. Her eyes widened, and she stuffed her hand into a pocket hidden in the matronly Alpine dress beneath her apron.

Zen, all the while, spoke German in that soft, compelling voice millions around the world loved to listen to on her vlogs. The woman focused on her as if she was an angel from heaven, and her expression turned to wonder. The woman then gestured and chattered with a jovial smile, as if she couldn't contain her excitement.

Zen bowed her thanks and turned to Bri and the others. "Frau Mueller said we can sit anywhere we want. The restaurant is usually busy, but everyone is at the grand opening. We also have permission to shoot. I convinced her it was free advertising to all the tourists who will be happily filling her place."

"Sitz, sitz." Frau Mueller smiled at them and then waved a finger at the gawking young woman and young man who were standing against the back wall.

Sally shrugged and led the way to a table next to the stone wall. She and Kristy settled in opposite each other and set their cameras up on short tripods and aimed them at themselves. Zen, sitting across from Bri in the outside seats, set up a small camera on a tripod and aimed it at her. Bri flashed a questioning look, and Zen ghosted a wink.

The young woman, dressed like a Bavarian barmaid—if the bar was a milk bar—delivered small steins of beer to the table. Unlike the older woman, she eyed them with great interest.

"I asked for their mildest beer to start," Zen said. "They also have sparkling water, some local soft drinks, and wine. Just let me know."

Kristy held up the mug. "Beer fits the place."

Sally nodded and lifted her mug.

Bri was not a big beer drinker but didn't mind it with certain foods and this certainly looked like a beer food type establishment. She raised her mug.

Zen grinned and held out her mug, and they clanked them together. "To new adventures and discoveries."

"To new adventures and discoveries," Bri intoned with the others and felt a little thrill about their illicit adventure. Maybe insisting that Sarah and Josh control everything wasn't always a good thing. Maybe spontaneous was okay . . . sometimes.

She watched with interest as the young man put a huge half round of cheese clasped in a metal contraption under a long metal box that seemed to act like a broiler. "What exactly is racl . . . whatever it's called?"

"Raclette is a type of cheese that is melted until it browns and then scraped onto a plate or a piece of bread," Zen said. "From Switzerland. It has an interesting smell. Some people find it a bit off-putting, but it tastes amazing. They serve it with boiled potatoes, pickled onions, and pickles. They'll also add ham or sausage."

Bri tried not to grimace. None of that sounded particularly appetizing. "Really?"

Zen cocked her head. "Do you like ham and cheese sandwiches?"

"Sure," Bri said.

"They also have a nice rustic bread and mustard." Zen nodded at a ceramic pot with a spoon sticking through a slit in the metal lid. "The mustard."

A few moments later, the young woman put a basket with a loaf of sliced crusty brown bread on the table.

"Oh my god. That smells amazing." Sally breathed in the aroma coming off the bread.

The grinning young woman returned with a tray of food. She put a dish of steaming small, boiled potatoes, a plate of pickled onions, and a plate of pickles in the middle of the table. She then put a small plate of ham in front of Bri.

Bri gave Zen a surprised look.

"I guessed you like ham better than sausage," Zen said.

"Good guess," Bri said, relieved. "I truly think sausage is one of man's more disgusting creations."

"In your Frankfurt vlog, you talked about the sausage but didn't include any footage of you actually tasting it," Zen said.

Sally and Kristy turned their attention to her.

"You've seen Bri's vlogs?" Sally asked.

Zen frowned. "I catch them and both of yours when I have the chance. Don't you watch each others' vlogs?"

Kristy shrugged. "Sure, when I have a chance."

Sally nodded. "Me, too."

The young woman returned with plates of the melted cheese for of each of them. She straightened and took a deep breath. "Please. Enjoy," she enunciated in English.

Zen smiled up at her. "Thank you." Then she said something in German.

The young woman beamed and almost skipped to a grinning Frau Mueller.

"What did you say?" Sally asked.

"I told her the food looks wonderful," Zen said.

Kristy speared a potato, scooped some onion and pickle onto her plate, and gathered a mouthful. "Let's give it a taste."

Zen was right about the smell, but Bri scraped a tiny bit of cheese onto her fork and tasted it. Not bad. She eyed the ham and the bread. After a day like today, a ham and cheese sandwich with pickle and potato on the side sounded better than a three Michelin star meal.

Zen put some potato, onion, pickle, and a slice of bread onto her plate and snapped a few photos of it with her phone and then made videos of the plate and the interior. She thumbed something into her phone and returned her attention to her meal. Bri remembered that Zen always posted photos of her meals to Instagram.

"This certainly beats the Marquardtian interpretation of the great American-style restaurant," Sally said.

Kristy smirked. "I wonder what the boys are eating."

Bri looked up from constructing her sandwich. "I wonder where Viktor thinks we are."

The others exchanged wide-eyed looks.

"Do you think Frau Mueller will get into trouble?" Bri asked in a low voice.

Zen shook her head. "Not if we have anything to say about it. I gave her my card and told her to blame us if she catches any grief for serving us."

Kristy waved her fork at Zen. "That was more than a card you gave her."

Zen shrugged. "Payment for this fine meal and a bit to help her transition to handling the crowds of tourists she's going to get after we sing her praises. Which means, they better not dare do anything but be proud of her and her restaurant."

"Never took you to be a rabble rouser"—Sally lifted her mug—"but I like it."

They all laughed. Bri was sure they were having a lot more fun than the others stuck with eating Marquardt's interpretation of family style American food in an eyesore of a building filled with drunk Marquardtians.

Zen

ZEN WALKED THE perimeter of the hotel's roof for the third time. Shame on them for not locking the access door. Safety seemed to be an afterthought in Marquardt. She felt a little better after running every floor and stairwell of the place—simply walking wasn't enough to burn off her excess energy and emotions. The building was five floors with two wings of rooms, so it only took her fifteen minutes to get to the roof.

She sighed as she gazed at the lights dancing on a distant snowy peak. They illuminated the original Alpine resort that had started the Benbrook dynasty over a century ago, and for the last fifty-seven years Marquardt had lost out on being a part of the network of walking/cross-country skiing/horseback riding trails that had been expanded and made popular by her family.

She had to figure out how to explain Marquardt to her aunt. She knew anything she said would trigger Fiona's strong chivalrous instinct to come charging in with her version of the cavalry and save this country from sliding into a poor, pitiful backwater instead of a place with a thriving tourist economy.

She smiled as she watched streams of light glide down the mountain from a cluster of lights near the resort. One of the many wonderful perks for Benbrook employees. A tradition as old as the resort itself—staff-only nighttime ski runs on a special patch of the mountain reserved for the Benbrook family and special guests.

She had her first major crush while skiing on that night lit slope. A sous chef she had barely noticed in the sea of white capped and aproned cooks in the kitchen had transformed into a funny, not to mention cute young woman in her ski parka . . .

Zen sighed and looked up at the stars. Not unlike a polished, slightly reserved travel vlogger who chose a tweed fedora to cover a rather quirky and increasingly endearing personality. A part of her had hoped her crush would be, well, crushed by meeting Bri face to face.

Well. She emitted a rueful laugh as she turned and strode to the stairwell door. *That certainly didn't happen.*

Bri

BRI WALKED OUT of the bathroom, feeling much better after a shower, and wrapped the hotel fluffy robe around her oversized sleep t-shirt. Zen was back and seated at the desk on her side of the room, pulling memory cards from her cameras.

"I bet they'll keep that back door locked after they find out we snuck back in through it." Bri gazed at her camera bag on the bed and sighed. All she wanted to do was go to sleep.

She had never thought about having to work after a day of working. Of course, that was what Sarah and Josh did when she retired to her room. She watched Zen doing her job without complaint.

Okay. She could do this. Everyone else was doing it tonight, and she certainly didn't want to be the last to get a vlog out. Oh no. This trip was a major battle for subscribers. She grabbed the bag and took it to the desk on her side of the huge wall television.

"I wonder if they have any fire regulations," Zen said.

Bri gave her a blank look.

"Locking the back door."

"Oh . . . Great. Something else to worry about." Bri removed her laptop from the bag and lined her cameras next to it . . . and just looked at them. Okay. First things first. She plugged the laptop into the convenient desktop power strip and powered it on. Josh had told her to upload the videos to the cloud. Instructions,

instructions. She unzipped several pockets and finally found her reporter's notebook.

"Do you need the password?" Zen asked.

Bri turned to her. "Password?"

"For the Internet."

"Right. Internet." Bri squinted at the icons on the home page. Josh or Sarah always set up her laptop in new places, and it automatically connected to the Internet at home because it was already set up. She wasn't a Luddite when it came to technology, she just never had a need to learn all the technical stuff beyond doing emails and making documents and using the Internet.

"It's a bit tricky here," Zen said. "Want me to do it?"

Trying not to look pathetically grateful, Bri stood, probably way too quickly, and stepped away from the seat. "Be my guest."

Wearing her patented benign smile that was mostly in her eyes, Zen slipped into Bri's chair and pulled down menus and typed in stuff after giving the screen a moment's glance. Her movements were both quick and steady in a graceful cadence. Bri could only stare, mesmerized. Who wouldn't be?

"Are you uploading your videos to a cloud?"

Bri blinked out of whatever weird spell she seemed to be under. "What?"

Zen looked back at her. "Cloud?"

"Oh, yes." Bri turned to the instructions page in her notebook and handed it to Zen.

Zen glanced at it, clicked on an icon, and did more typing at lightning speed.

"Wow," Bri muttered, "you're hired."

Zen flicked an amused grin at her. "I see a folder has been prepared for this trip."

"It has?" Bri looked over Zen's shoulder. A folder named Marquardt was in a window. Zen opened the folder, revealing several more folders marked Day 1, Day 2, through Day 7. Josh really had thought of everything.

Zen opened Day 1. "There you go." She stood and went back to her desk.

"Thanks," Bri said as she settled into the chair.

She stared at the screen. The videos. She had to get them off the memory cards. She picked up the main camera and carefully removed the SD card. She felt along the side of the computer for the slot and finally got the card in after flipping it around several times.

She watched the screen for something to happen. An icon appeared. That must be it. She waited. After a few seconds, she got the feeling it was waiting for her.

"I should get your videos from my cameras onto your computer."

Bri whipped her head to Zen so fast, she was lucky she didn't snap anything. Zen held up three memory cards.

"Good idea." Bri stood, hoping she didn't look too eager or relieved, and parked herself in the easy chair next to the desk.

Zen slipped into Bri's chair and opened an icon. "I'm going to create a folder on your computer for the files on your memory card, so I can pop it out and put mine in."

Bri pushed down her panic on how much she didn't know what she was supposed to do. "Go for it." She tried to sound nonchalant.

Zen created a folder, then clicked on the icon that had appeared when Bri had inserted the memory card. It opened, and Zen grabbed all the files at once and dragged them into the new folder. She popped out Bri's card and inserted one of hers. She moved the files to the new folder. She opened each of the other cards and put them on image view and moved over select videos.

Bri leaned closer. How could she tell which files were which just by looking at the thumbnail?

"So your editor knows what's what, I'll put together a little spreadsheet matching description with the video file number." Zen's fingers and eyes never stopped moving as she opened a blank spreadsheet and named it Marquardt Day 1 plus the date, copied in filenames, and typed in the place, the activity, and a description in brief phrases.

"How do you know what's on each video?" Bri asked.

Zen glanced back. "We didn't do much today so it's pretty easy to remember. Each camera has a different type of filename, so you used the little camera in the lobby"—she pointed to several thumbnails that clearly showed the crowd of locals—"and you used it on our restaurant adventure." She continued to explain the thumbnails as she copied and pasted and typed. "I also donated some B-roll from the village in Austria, from inside the bus, and when we got off the bus your editor might want to splice in for continuity."

Zen added the thumbnails Bri had shot with her camera to the spreadsheet and sorted all the videos into chronological order. "Saves explaining the order of activities to your editor. Then all you have to do is write up your notes."

Bri sucked in her breath. "Voice over. I've prerecorded the introduction to the series but . . ."

Zen looked at Bri's equipment. "You can plug that microphone into the computer and record."

Bri eyed the microphone, realizing she couldn't fake her way out of this any longer. "It's just . . ." She sighed and sank into the cushy chair.

Zen turned her chair around and waited with a calm patience as if she had all the time in the world.

Bri stared across the room at the darkness outside the window. "I thought this would be easy . . . I mean I've been vlogging for seven years."

Zen leaned forward and clasped her hands together. "Vlogging is entertainment, and we all have our behind-the-scenes things to create the illusion of what becomes our persona."

Bri crossed her arms. "Are you going to tell me you don't walk everywhere?"

Zen gave a half shrug. "I admit I do walk everywhere, except on very rare occasions when safety or a time commitment means I have to take transportation for as short a distance as possible. And, of course, when I have to cross a large body of water."

Bri nodded. "And you always say when you have to do that."

"Because of my challenge to myself to keep within my own parameters," Zen said. "But I do stay at establishments owned or operated by my family and with friends whenever possible. Which is why I never show or do reviews of places I sleep at."

"But you shoot your own video and say your own words." Bri put her face into her hands, feeling overwhelmed and way over her head. How did she ever think she could do this on her own?

Zen picked up the microphone and plugged it into the computer, then brought up a program that looked like a sound studio. She held the microphone out to Bri.

Bri lowered her hands and stared at the microphone. Against her better judgement, she took it.

Zen turned back to the computer and opened the first video on her spreadsheet. Bri watched as the village appeared on the screen. "It doesn't look as bad as when I was shooting it," she said, amazed.

"It didn't feel like a promising beginning to an adventure we're all a little apprehensive about." Zen clicked on another video following the train from the air as it arrived at the station.

Bri stared at the screen. Wow. The footage was of her and the others getting off the train. Then it swept into the town, revealing ancient buildings clinging to a hill, looking much more interesting than from the ground.

Bri pulled the chair closer and leaned forward. "Whoa. How did you get that?"

"I put my drone up when I was walking to the village."

"Won't you use it?"

"I have several drone clips of the town," Zen said.

Bri frowned. "You'll just let me have it?"

Zen turned to her. "Sure. You have more use for it than I do."

"But . . ." Bri gave her head a shake. Zen was the rival for solo traveling supremacy. The one person she felt in direct competition with. Could she really be the gentle Buddha-like woman who trod softly as she presented the world as a beautiful place filled with kind and good people?

"For your voice over, just talk about your impressions as you look at the videos. Record in segments, match the audio segments to the video clips and let your editor tighten them up."

Zen made it sound so easy. Josh and Sarah made it look so easy, and Bri had been beyond delusional to think she could do it.

"Start the audio with the file name of the video clip, so you just have to record the segments and upload them. Just say, 'For filename whatever it is,' and then do your narrative."

Bri calmed down her panic. That didn't sound so hard. She could do that. "How does the program work?"

Zen showed Bri how to make and save the recordings and how to put them in the folder on her computer. Bri did two recordings and by the third one, she didn't need any prompting from Zen. She surprised herself by thinking of things to say that sounded as good as anything Sarah fed her. *Maybe I can do this.*

"When you have all your recordings, close this window like this"—Zen closed the window, leaving an icon—"grab the folder and drag it into the cloud window. It's a lot of stuff, so it'll take time for all of it to upload." She stood. "That's it."

Zen returned to her own computer, glancing back a couple of times.

Bri sat in front of her computer and turned to Zen. "Thank you."

Zen shrugged. "No problem."

"No, really," Bri said. "You don't have to help me. You've got your own work to do."

"My sister, Karma, actually has the tougher job, making sense of the mess of stuff I send her," Zen said.

Bri shook her head, frustrated. "I mean, we're all here vying for viewers of this first glimpse of Marquardt. Since I'm basically here under false pretenses because I only pretend to be a solo traveler, I wouldn't blame you if you just said tough luck."

Zen gazed at her with a gentle puzzled expression. "First off, you *present* as a solo traveler. Not pretend. Second, we're not in a competition. We're here to experience a new place and share our experience with people who watch each of our vlog channels."

Bri stared at her, trying to see below the gentle calm exterior. This was easy for her to say with over four million followers, but something stopped her from saying it out loud. She looked into those eyes—kind of an amazing gray—and couldn't do it. Unlike all the other vloggers, including herself, Zen never asked people to subscribe to her channel or sold merchandise or had sponsors that offered viewers discounts for products. She didn't even use her family name or connections. She got her followers on the merits of her vlogs alone.

"So"—Bri took a deep breath—"we'll just keep this between us?"

Zen grinned. "Of course. Just watch me and others for reminders to shoot and talk to the camera and you'll do fine."

Zen

ZEN BREATHED IN the chilly night air. She had always loved nighttime in the mountains. She slumped into the patio seat on the balcony off her room. Karma's face filled her phone propped up on a round table. Karma was multi-tasking as usual, her video equipment and large screens flickering with footage taking up the wall behind her. Her assistants were already putting together Zen's latest vlog.

"Sounds like you had an interesting day." Karma, master of understatement, couldn't keep away an amused grin. "You even survived meeting your massive crush."

Zen sighed as she gazed at the crescent moon.

"Still have a crush, now that you've met her?" Karma glanced back at a screen. The aerial footage of them getting off the bus was being edited. Bri was pulling her case away while fending off Viktor's attempts to help.

Zen smiled at the footage. "Yeah."

Karma shook her head. "Don't get yourself heartbroken."

"At least I have a chance with her."

"But it's complicated by her not being out," Karma said.

Zen shrugged. "I'm willing to risk it."

Karma gave her a knowing look. "You say in your patented calm and blasé way." She shook her finger at Zen. "Just take care of that soft heart of yours. You're running out of long walks to make it whole again."

"The last woman to truly break my heart was Emily." Zen sat up. "I was twenty-one and stupid."

"Now you're twice that age and not any smarter. With a life of avoiding relationship commitments so you won't go through that again." Karma looked at something in front of her and turned to the side. "Let that scene linger for a few more seconds." She spun her chair back to Zen. "I hope she's worth it, for your sake."

"I don't have a choice." Zen stared at what was left of the moon as it disappeared behind a whisp of clouds. "I know it's crazy. But . . ." She threw up her hands.

"Just be careful, little sis," Karma said. "I don't want to explain you melting down from a broken heart to Aunt Fiona, especially when she expects you to get Marquardt for her."

Zen sighed. "I very reluctantly agreed to help her."

Karma laughed. "Master of understatement. I know you would have gotten out of it if you could have."

"You know, now that I see the damage Fitz has caused, I'm determined to help get this country on the right track."

Karma grinned. "Once a Benbrook always a Benbrook."

Zen smiled as she signed off and stared for a few more minutes at the illuminated spire of a church on a low hill rising from the other side of town. She sucked in one last breath of cool air, opened the sliding glass door, and stepped into the dusky room.

Bri was a dark lump on the bed closest to the bathroom. Zen stilled and watched her sleep before snapping herself out of it. Too stalkerish. Gotta watch that.

Zen sighed as she gazed at Bri again. This was either going to be the best or the worst week of her life.

5
Day Two — Morning
Bri

BRI AND ZEN turned the corner to the lobby and stopped. No sign that it had been an aging Teutonic mosh pit the night before. In fact, no sign of anyone at all. Not even at the service counter.

Bri glanced around. "We're the first ones up?"

"Maybe the others are in the restaurant," Zen said.

"They *did* promise twenty-four-seven."

Their footfalls echoed as they walked across the lobby. Too loudly. Bri feared Viktor was lurking about just waiting to pounce on them and ask where they had been last night. Zen had sounded very reasonable when they thought it might be a good idea to get their story straight. She said to tell the truth. Viktor never told them they couldn't go anywhere—his weird reaction to Sally's wandering away aside. And he never said eating in the hotel restaurant was mandatory. Bri's reasonable mind completely agreed with this while the unreasonable part didn't want to explain it to a very agitated Viktor.

Another set of footfalls started following them, and Bri spun around, heart pounding. She let out a relieved breath. Just Joe the Historian. And he was wearing a wry grin.

"So, we all believed Viktor when he was sure you guys were so exhausted from your travels, not to mention missing your husbands, to join us for dinner."

Bri and Zen exchanged shocked looks.

"Imagine my surprise when I get a notification on my phone, and I see an Instagram post of a plate of raclette and then another post of the interior of a quaint restaurant." He put his hands on his hips.

"We found the vegetarian menu less than satisfactory," Zen said.

"So, Viktor thinks . . . ?" Bri prompted.

"He thinks you stayed in your rooms and got room service," Joe said.

Bri gave him a wary look. "And what is he going to continue to think?"

Joe put up his hands, laughing. "We decided not to rat on you. We may need a return favor while we're here."

Bri relaxed and tried to look as if it was no big deal. Inside, she was on her knees in thanks to whatever entity was willing to listen to her.

"You *are* going to have to tell us where this place is," Joe said as they continued to the restaurant.

"Frau Mueller will be disappointed if you don't visit," Zen said.

They walked into the restaurant and stopped at the host stand. The place was a lot larger and cavernous than Bri had imagined. At least the décor was more hotel dining room than American family-style restaurant. The aromas from the kitchen smacked her in her very empty stomach.

"Where's Viktor?" Bri asked.

"He's buzzing around." Joe nodded to the young man in a blindingly white shirt and black slacks at the host stand.

He straightened and stepped around the stand. "This way, please," he said in careful English.

They followed him past several tables to a buffet setup in the middle of the room, a pair of matronly women in white aprons standing behind it. Of course, food was women's work. Their eyes were on the food trays. They were probably warned not to stare or show their disapproval of the loose foreign women.

The young man put his hand out to a round table set for eight.

"Thank the gods," Zen breathed.

Bri turned to her.

She nodded at the buffet. "We can see the food and select accordingly."

"Ah." Bri settled into a seat across from her.

"Guess we should see what they're serving." Joe stood and went to the end of the buffet table.

Zen inspected a metal pot and poured hot water into her cup. She thumbed through an assortment of tea bags in a woven basket on the table and selected English Breakfast.

Bri peeked into the tall white carafe. Coffee. She didn't even care if it was terrible . . . well, maybe a little. She filled her cup. Zen stirred milk and sugar into her tea as she studied the buffet table.

"See anything edible?" Bri took a sip of the coffee. Not too bad.

"Some possibilities." Zen stood. "Time to forage."

Bri joined her at the buffet table and grabbed a plate. Zen selected several hunks of melon and oranges, a couple slices of rustic brown bread, and two soft boiled eggs. Bri scooped some scrambled egg onto her plate, picked up two slices of toast, and some kind of hash browns or German potato pancake.

She headed back to the table as Mick, Jon, and George scooted into their seats.

Mick looked at their plates. "Looks halfway edible."

"Hard to mess up breakfast." Joe picked up a maple syrup dispenser and sniffed it. He poured some over a stack of American-style pancakes.

Sally and Kristy approached the table.

"The gang's all here," Sally said as she went straight to the buffet table and grabbed a plate. "And I'm starved."

Kristy laughed as she sat down. "Coffee first."

Bri relaxed a bit, surrounded by a group she had always thought of as her competitors and now . . . Now, they were more like comrades in arms. The others were trading hilarious and horrific breakfast stories, almost making it feel like a bunch of solo travelers who found themselves in some random out-in-the-middle-of-nowhere place at the same time. For all their cheerfulness, Bri could feel the nervous apprehension beneath their chatter. She didn't think any of them were really looking forward to today with excited anticipation.

Zen was being her quiet calm self. She listened to the others as she ate her interesting mix of food with two more trips to the buffet table. She seemed to be soaking in everything without actually being a part of it. But she was not aloof. If anything, she exuded a quiet engagement with those around her—the definition of a good listener. Given Zen's job before she had decided to travel the world on foot, this ability to listen and soak up a culture was something she had to be really good at.

Zen lifted her cup of tea to her lips and ghosted a wink at Bri.

Bri blinked at her and stared down at the remnants on her plate. A complex personality simmered beneath Zen's reserved calm that Bri was getting way too curious about. She gave her head a shake as she picked up her coffee cup. Zen was her main competition. She had to stop having these weird thoughts about her.

"Excuse me."

They all turned to a nervous-looking young man. He stared at them wide-eyed, probably startled he got their attention so fast.

"Greetings, travelers," he said in precise but accented English. "I am Albert, Viktor's assistant. Viktor hopes you had a good night's sleep and a good breakfast. He invites you to meet him outside the front doors at nine-thirty for your first adventure in Marquardt."

He hesitated, then bowed his head and walk-ran to the door.

"I hope this week is more than controlled sightseeing," Mick said.

Joe sat forward and put his elbows on the table. "We'll just have to make it clear that good reviews come from allowing us the freedom to discover the place on our own."

George cocked his head. "But will they let regular tourists just roam around?"

"If they don't, they're going to be surprised when people decide not to visit." Mick put his napkin on his plate.

"I wasn't expecting to be a part of a political experiment." Sally took a deep breath. "But it sounds like it could be fun."

Bri

THE GLASS DOORS whooshed open to the brisk mountain air. Viktor was standing in front of a small tourist van with another smaller van behind it. They, at least, looked as if they had been built in the last decade or so. Bri put herself behind John and Mick as they walked across the threshold. Zen gave her an amused look as she aimed her camera at the scene in front of them. In fact, everyone had their cameras out, ready to record.

Zen sidled over to Bri and held out two oranges. "For you. I swiped a few from the buffet table."

Surprised, Bri took the oranges. "Thank you."

"I always try to keep some fruit in my camera bag because you never know when the next meal will be."

"Good thinking." Bri slipped the oranges into her backpack.

Viktor, enthusiastic smile in place, clasped his hands together. "Good morning, good morning." He squinted at them as if making sure they were all present. "Today we have an exciting tour lined up. We are going to our most ancient landmark, Fort Trotz. It has protected us from invaders through the centuries and it represents our independent spirit."

Okay, off to a good start. Bri exchanged optimistic looks with the others.

"For the ladies, we have a very special treat." Viktor beamed in Bri's direction.

For the ladies . . . ?

"You get to be the first to try our state-of-the-art spa," Viktor said, "spending the morning being pampered."

What . . . ?

"Spas aren't my thing," Kristy said. "I want to see the fort."

Viktor stared startled at her. "Oh . . . oh. The spa is more appropriate."

"Spas are disgusting," Sally muttered.

Bri straightened. "I don't go any place that involves personal hygiene without extensive research and health reports."

Everyone turned to Zen. She shook her head, turned, and strode in her easy gait to the side road.

"Wait, wait." Viktor stumbled several steps after Zen, but she had already rounded the corner of the hotel toward town. He turned to the others, looking flustered.

Jon bounced on the balls of his feet. "I love spas. I wouldn't mind trying out your new facilities."

Viktor's eyes grew so wide, Bri feared he'd hurt them. "Oh, that wouldn't be possible." He vigorously shook his head. "Only ladies work there."

Jon shrugged. "As with most spas I've been to."

Viktor looked as if he was about to combust from shock. He worked to compose himself. "They are prepared for you ladies at the spa."

"It'll be good practice for when people cancel appointments," Kristy said.

"They have special things prepared for our special guests," Viktor said. "Special, special women things. They're all excited to impress you."

Bri could only imagine what those special things could be. Or maybe not, given the century and decade they seemed to be living in.

Sally put her hands on her hips. "Look. One of the few things I could research about this country is the fort, so I'm really looking forward to seeing the forty-foot-tall twelfth-century turret, the replica of the trebuchet from the fourteenth century, and, most of all, the collection of swords."

"And don't forget the unique way the wall is built into the cliffside," Kristy said.

Viktor stared at them, mouth open.

Bri shouldered her pack and walked to the van. "I'm excited to see this piece of history." She climbed the steps as Viktor sputtered his protest behind her.

The others clambered up the steps behind Bri, chattering at their cameras and sitting in any spare seat.

Viktor, muttering on his phone, scrambled onto the van and faced seven cameras aimed at him. He disconnected the phone. "This van isn't big enough."

George looked around. "There're still empty seats."

"Not big enough for proper seating," Viktor said, exasperated. "You shouldn't be sitting next to a woman."

George looked across the aisle at Kristy. He stood and crossed his arms. "What were you learning when you spent a year joining the twenty-first century?"

Viktor blinked at him. Blank, uncomprehending. "We've been very diligent in our study of the world around us."

"Obviously not diligent enough." George sat down.

Didn't he really get it? Or maybe the new progressive president wasn't as progressive as the platform he had run on. Of course, promising things to get into office was a whole lot easier than actually getting those things done, especially if he had to change beliefs that seemed to be so ingrained they were almost chiseled in stone.

Viktor looked them over again with a resigned expression and sat in the seat next to the driver. He nodded at the driver, who put the van in gear and eased it onto the road that went toward town and then skirted around it, since the cobblestone lane they had taken to the restaurant last night was too narrow for vehicles.

"Wondering where Zen is?" Mick asked in a low voice after about fifteen minutes of a relatively smooth ride.

Bri and the others glanced back at Viktor, who was muttering into his phone.

"Instagram."

They put down their cameras and pulled out their phones. Bri went to Zen's Instagram feed and stared at a photo of Zen on a narrow dirt trail in a grassy field on the side of a mountain. How did she get wherever she was so fast? The caption read: "The magic of Marquardt begins with the bucolic fields, which are crisscrossed with trails that make great scenic shortcuts to what will be the biggest tourist spots."

A second photo—taken from what looked halfway up the mountain—was of the town nestled in the tiny valley, looking quaint and inviting. Zen had caught it sparkling in the morning sun. More importantly, the shot did not include the hotel or any of the modern parts of the town.

"Damn," Sally muttered. "She's having all the fun."

Joe sputtered a laugh. "If she's where I think she is, we'll be seeing her soon."

Kristy looked out the window as they turned off onto a sketchy-looking narrow road. "Really?"

Bri peeked out the window as they eased toward a switchback clinging to the edge of a steep drop off. *Oh, my god.* She closed her eyes and turned away from the window.

Zen

WELL, THAT DIDN'T last long. Zen strode past the cobblestone lane that was the only way into the maze of lanes because of the wall around the old town. Sorry, Aunt Fiona. She trotted on the paved road that followed the south wall of the town, forcing herself to not push into a full run.

Did they really think women wouldn't be interested in visiting a fort? Or that they wanted to go to a country not known for its hot springs and then spend all their time in a spa? Even Fiona couldn't have envisioned this level of cluelessness when Marquardt had agreed to Fitz's stupid ideas. Fitz was only about taking the money and run, not whether something was the right thing to do.

She glanced back at the glass monstrosity on top of the hill. She hated that she left Bri to deal with such an inane situation. On the other hand, Bri probably could handle it. Her television reporter background came through in her vlogs when she had to defuse the occasional awkward situation they all ran into sometimes.

The road headed toward the small mountain in front of her. She could just see the famous turret attached to the fort above the trees at the top of the mountain. She jogged past the few buildings outside the town walls. One wooden building next to the road had a sign that all but shouted "men-only drinking establishment." She had no doubt beer flowed like a river in Marquardt—the only acceptable way of living under an oppressive regime.

A gravel and dirt road met the paved one. Zen stopped and studied the fields rising up from the mountain side of the road. Cows were scattered about, munching the new shoots of grass and wildflowers. Also . . . a trail. She cocked her head and squinted at a rocky section. Yep. A well-kept trail.

"I'll wager a hundred euros it goes all the way to the fort." She grinned and strode onto the gravel road.

Bri

BRI STUDIED THE latest photo Zen had posted to take her mind off the van lurching and leaning in the wrong direction. Zen was walking up the steep path with an expression of delight as she gazed at something above her. Only Zen could make what was certainly a rigorous trek look like an inviting leisurely stroll. The Marquardt authorities would never be able to keep the tourists off those mountain trails. Like they didn't have an inkling that Zen's fanatical followers of walking tourists were already booking their way to Marquardt at that moment.

The van slowed and rocked a little too much and the braver of the travelers aimed cameras out the windows on the precarious edge side. They all held their breaths through a too tight hairpin curve. Bri was certain half the van was hanging off the edge.

"I'm going back with Zen," Sally said through gritted teeth as she gripped the seat in front of her.

"Sounds like a great plan." Mick almost dropped his camera as they hit a pothole too hard.

Bri clutched the back of the seat in front of her, trying to catch her breath. No one said anything about life-threatening dangerous roads. Life-threatening dangerous drivers were bad enough.

"Viktor, sir." George, who was closest to the front, sat forward.

Viktor turned around. "Yes. What can I do for you?"

"Will you be putting in railings and fixing the potholes before tourists are allowed on this road?"

Viktor's eyes widened at all the cameras aimed at him. "We plan to shuttle tourists up to the fort."

"Regardless, are you putting in railings and fixing the potholes for the shuttles?" George asked in a patient voice he probably perfected when he taught high school before he became a bookstore owner.

Viktor straightened. "Our drivers are the best. They can drive this road with no problem."

"Regardless, it doesn't do you any good to give tourists an uncomfortable at the least and terrifying at the most experience."

George pulled his glasses down his nose and leveled his teacher gaze at Viktor.

The van slowed and then lurched and swayed around another v-shaped curve, with added exaggerated bumps for drama. Bri closed her eyes, trying not to envision the tires halfway off the edge. Thank god Zen had convinced her to wear her most comfortable walking shoes. No way was she going to get in this van to go downhill. She'd hire a helicopter to rescue her if she had to.

Viktor frowned. "Tourists like adventure tours. With a little excitement."

Jon stood up and braced himself as he swayed between the seats. "They expect all safety precautions have been made or they expect to be told about the dangers and to sign a waiver showing they understand what they're getting into. None of us would have gotten on this van if we knew the conditions of this road and the lack of railings on the edge of the drop-offs."

Viktor's expression cleared of its puzzlement. "I understand. You're concerned about the women. How many women are going to be interested in visiting a military fort?"

Sally threw up her hands. "All of them. Its history, its architecture, it most likely has a great view and, I hear you have an armory with some eleventh-century swords, which are a special interest of mine. Seeing them is almost worth this perilous trip."

Viktor blinked at her as if she'd spoken Klingon.

The van shifted around another bend onto a flat expanse. Bri gazed out the window at an ancient wall of stone with a towering fat turret rising up from the rocky landscape.

They all released their breaths as the van shuddered to a stop.

Viktor stood and clasped his hands together. "Welcome to the legendary Fort Trotz." He pushed the door open, and they all clambered out.

Bri took in a deep breath of the cool air. Mountain air. She lifted her camera on the selfie stick and said, "The first thing that hits me is the cool mountain air." *Easy. Just say what comes to mind.*

The others around her were recording their first impressions. Someone in what looked like a medieval military show costume—not remotely practical for actual battle—was shouting and gesturing from the open gate in the wall. Viktor met him halfway across the grass and a loud, wild discussion of waving arms and lots of pointing toward the fort ensued.

Joe stepped up next to Bri. "Wonder what Zen has done."

Bri turned to him surprised and then returned her attention to Viktor. Something glistened halfway down the wall. She squinted as it moved into a shadow. A small drone. She couldn't help grinning. She knew one thing Zen was doing. The drone lifted and disappeared on the other side of the wall, and she felt a momentary void. Just seeing Zen's drone had raised her spirits a bit.

She glanced around at her colleagues. They were busy shooting and talking, while keeping an eye on Viktor. Bri couldn't help admiring Zen's quiet rebellious attitude. She wished she had half the guts to say screw this and go off on her own adventure.

Viktor ended his spirited tirade, and the hapless young man jumped out of the way as Viktor stomped to the gate.

"I think we should see what's up." Kristy didn't wait for a consensus as she strode toward the fort.

"Especially if it has to do with Zen." George followed Kristy.

"One for all and all for one." Mick flourished an imaginary sword as the rest of them trotted to the gate.

Bri

BRI TOOK IN the good-sized courtyard surrounded by walls that looked like they could have been built yesterday, except for the worn aging of the stone. She had read that Fort Trotz never had to be used for defense because no one had ever bothered to attack the tiny country.

Zen was sitting cross-legged on a low wall, looking as calm as her name. Men in those showy medieval uniforms—surprisingly feminine-looking by twenty-first-century patriarchy standards— were watching her from a safe distance as if she was a bizarre, dangerous beast.

"Love the frilly white shirts," Kristy said.

Sally nodded. "Nothing says manly man like a long, upturned shoe with a squashed tennis ball over the toes."

Viktor stomped to Zen and placed himself at about the same distance as the other men. "You can't walk off like that." He waved his hands. His English probably wasn't good enough to convey his extreme frustration.

Zen looked up from manipulating the control in her hands.

Bri looked around for the drone. It was hovering nearby. She put her hand over her mouth to stop a laugh. The others all had their cameras on the scene from different perspectives as close as possible without being obtrusive. She lifted her camera and moved to get a good view of both Zen and Viktor.

"Sure, I can. In fact, I did," Zen said.

"Yes, yes. You did." Viktor vigorously nodded. "But you can't. Not again."

Zen cocked her head. "Are you saying it's dangerous to be out alone in your country?"

Viktor stumbled back, his expression comical in its shock. The show soldiers exchanged startled glances. Some even gasped in dismay.

"Dangerous? No, no. Marquardt is very safe. Very very safe."

"So, if not dangerous, why shouldn't I be allowed to walk around alone?" Zen took a deep breath and uncrossed her legs.

"To protect you." Viktor sounded exasperated. "Your reputation."

Zen looked up at the sky and shook with laughter.

Jon scratched behind his ear. "Guess Zen doesn't need our help."

"Reputation." Viktor narrowed his eyes. "The vehicle that brought you here, was there a woman in it? Did you sit in the back seat?"

Zen grinned as she hopped off the wall, forcing Viktor to step back.

"He should not have picked you up, but he also could not allow you to be walking alone, so he did the honorable thing." Viktor seemed to be waging a major moral war with his own dilemmas. "But he should have taken you back to the hotel. How could he have dropped you off up here as if this was a proper destination for a woman . . . ?"

Zen shrugged and walked to Bri and the other travelers.

Viktor turned around, looking shocked that Zen simply strolled away in the middle of his rant. "I must know who brought you here."

Zen crossed her arms. "No one gave me a ride."

Viktor stared at her and then emitted a nervous laugh. "Yes. Humor. Funny."

Zen shrugged. "I can't help if you don't believe me."

Viktor mimicked her crossed arms. "Okay then. You're here, so how did you get here?" He looked around with a "gotcha" smirk.

The show soldiers laughed and nudged each other.

"The way I get everywhere," Zen said.

Viktor frowned, then sighed. "Yes. Your gimmick is you walk everywhere. Now how did you really get here?"

"I walked."

"Impossible." Viktor waved at the gate. "It's thirteen kilometers. Eight kilometers up the mountain alone."

"Which is why the road is not the best way to get here . . . for many reasons," Zen said. "Not the way my followers will take."

Viktor frowned. "It's the only way for visitors."

"The walk past town is less than a half a kilometer. Another half a kilometer beyond that is a farm road that goes around the bottom of this mountain. About a quarter kilometer down this road is a nice three-and-a-half-kilometer trail through cow fields and open grasslands that ends in the back of the fort. Lovely walk." Zen flashed a grin at Bri. "My Instagram followers are already planning trips to be the first to walk your rather extensive trail system."

Viktor stared, confused. "Trail system?"

"You have few roads and not many motor vehicles," Zen said. "The roads are mostly unpaved, so you have lots of trails. Your main transportation is foot, horse, bicycle, scooter, sledge, snowmobile, skis . . ."

"Oh my." Viktor actually slapped his hand to his chin. "People walking around all over the place?"

"If you didn't want walkers, why did you invite me to promote your country?" Zen asked. "If not to promote your country as a part of the established walking trail system throughout these mountains."

"Brilliant," Joe muttered.

Viktor emitted a nervous laugh. "It's just a show. Entertainment. You don't really walk everywhere."

Zen turned to the other travelers. "If you guys want to walk back, I'll be around to show the way." She raised a jaunty eyebrow at Bri.

Bri and the others could only stare as she strode through the open gate.

Sally held out her phone to Viktor. "This is what Zen posted to Instagram today. It already has nine thousand likes and four thousand comments on it and many from people wanting to know how to get here, where to stay, wanting to see more places to walk . . ."

Viktor stared at the screen as Sally scrolled through the endless comments.

Sally shook her head at his uncomprehending look. "This is why you invited all of us. To get people interested in visiting here. We each have our unique points of view with our own like-minded followers, and we're going to be presenting this place through those points of view. But we won't be able to if we're not allowed the freedom we have everywhere else in Europe. The more you restrict us, the harder it is for us to show our followers what a great place this is to visit."

Viktor waved his finger at her. "I need to be having this conversation with your husband. He understands the business behind all this."

Sally threw up her hands. "My followers want to see those swords. Anyone want to join me?"

"You bet," George said as Bri and the others followed Sally to what looked like the main entrance of the fort proper.

Sally stopped and looked back. "Is someone going to show us where they are?"

Viktor snapped out of his shock and gestured at a young man in a very foppish red hat.

Something glistened in the sun near the wall. Zen was certainly having fun. Bri hoped she got Sally's exchange with Viktor.

Zen

ZEN WALKED AROUND to the north side of the fort to a green spot with stone benches. She stopped in the middle of it and spun around. Nice space. Perfect place for a couple of food kiosks and tables. She studied the fort wall and walked to the edge of the grass that overlooked the deep narrow valley with a rollicking river snaking through it.

She knew the land on the other side of the river as well as any local, having spent several summers working in the family resort in Italy just a few miles away. Food. She grinned as she pulled out her phone. Since none of her colleagues seemed keen on going back on the bus, they'd need lunch. More importantly, Bri will be hungry.

Fortunately, her cousin Leez was the manager of the restaurant concessions at the resort. She scrolled through her contacts and hit a number. "Hey, Leez. Up for some fun?"

Bri

BRI WAS KIND of thankful for the opportunity to leisurely walk around a place with so many things to shoot. She could relax a little and take the time to frame a shot, linger on a scene. She zoomed in on details of the uncomfortable-looking armor and ancient weapons. She read the little signs—written in German, French, Italian, English, Spanish, and what looked like Japanese—and combined this information with her own reactions to what she was shooting as she talked to the camera. She even remembered Zen's advice to use all the senses if she needed something to focus on. Like the musty odor and faint animal smell.

The travelers stuck together, forming their own little tour group. Bri certainly didn't want to get caught alone and having to face Viktor or one of the many young show soldiers, who didn't look happy about having to explain their assigned sections of the fort to a group that included women. They really needed to work on a larger repertoire of facial expressions beyond dour and hostile.

They ran into the little issue of no women's restroom, because, of course, why would women want to visit a fort? But the guys gallantly guarded the door as Bri, Kristy, and Sally used the men's facilities, which were super clean with fresh paint and modern fixtures. They decided to make sure whoever was in charge of preparing sites for tourists to know they had to add an equally fine women's restroom to the fort.

Bri had to admit, the expression on the young man's face when Sally peppered him with questions about the swords: forging techniques, composition of metals . . . very specific information and questions using all the jargon, was going to go viral. The man kept darting glances at the guys as if they needed to stop this woman from talking. But the guys were just watching him, waiting for him to answer Sally's questions. He hemmed and hawed and then turned to the guys and continued his obviously memorized speech about the swords.

Sally had done a great job of holding in her anger. Ancient weaponry was a serious pursuit for her as a part of her job as a movie stunt woman. Did they really not do their homework about each of them? Bri could still feel Sally simmering as they emerged from the torchlit dark-stoned interior of the fort into the midday sun.

Mick looked around. "Wonder where Viktor is."

George adjusted his pack on his shoulders. "Gives us a chance to make our escape without having a confrontation."

"Smart thinking."

"He could be waiting at the van," Kristy said.

Joe nodded at a side door into the fort. "I saw another way out."

"Excellent," George said. "Lead on."

The show soldiers lounging around the courtyard watched them but didn't seem overly anxious to care about what they were up to. They definitely needed to work on their hospitality skills.

Bri followed the others back into the dark of the fort, down a narrow corridor with a half-opened door at the end. Joe put his shoulder to the door, and it creaked open wider. They pressed through the doorway and streamed onto a delightful patch of green with benches around the edges, like a little park.

They turned in circles and laughed. The green space was the friendliest, most inviting thing Bri had seen so far in this strange country. The area was almost magical in the sparkling mountain air. She joined the others in shooting and talking to the cameras as they walked to the edge of the grass that faced snow-capped mountains rising above them from the deep narrow gorge. She leaned over the rather dramatic cliff to get a shot of the fort wall that looked as if it sprouted up from the rock. She straightened and looked the other way where a trail followed the edge of the cliff as it dwindled down to the valley floor.

She blinked at a movement through a cluster of trees. Several people were trekking up the trail clinging to the edge of the cliff. As they got closer, Bri recognized a familiar rust-colored t-shirt, light jacket, and distinctive hiking pants.

"Is that Zen?" she asked.

The others wandered to her and shaded their eyes as they looked down the trail.

"How'd she make friends already?" Joe scratched his head.

Whoever they were, they seemed to be as fit as Zen because they were climbing up the trail like it was a cornfield in North Dakota. They were also carrying white bags.

"Gotta admit, she knows how to create her own adventure," Sally said.

Zen and a pair of young women topped the cliff and winnowed their way through the long blowing grass. Zen's companions wore burgundy long-sleeved T-shirts with a Double B logo on them. Definitely not Marquardtians.

"Hi," Zen said as they stepped onto the trimmed grass. "Isn't this a great space?"

They all kind of stared at her, as if showing up with a couple of strangers who weren't locals was no big deal.

"Are you going to introduce us to your friends?" Kristy asked.

Zen turned to the grinning young women. "This is my cousin, Leez, and her friend Rosie. They work in the resort just beyond that bend in the valley." She pointed to where the valley rose and then disappeared around the mountain. "I didn't see a food vendor up here, so I gave Leez a call to see if she was up for a bit of an adventure."

Zen, Leez, and Rosie put the canvas bags imprinted with the Double-B logo on the ground and pulled out bulging white paper bags.

"The vegetarian ones are marked with a V," Zen said.

Bri and the others stared, mouths hanging open at this completely unexpected and extremely welcomed surprise. The oranges Zen had given her had been sacrificed to her stomach too long ago.

"How did you do this in such a short amount of time?" Mick asked.

Zen turned to the valley. "The border is the river until you get to the bend, then it curves this way into Marquardt and Italy is the other way. The resort is maybe a mile beyond the bend and there's a road that follows the river on the Italian side. I put in the order for some sandwiches and met Leez and Rosie down at the old bridge across the river. The road is blocked on the Marquardt side but the bridge is walkable."

Sally grinned. "Door Dash, Italian style."

Jon picked up a bag and looked inside. "Two bottles of water. Bless you a million times over."

"I also noticed the lack of water fountains or urns," Zen said.

George looked around. "As nice as this place is, I don't want to explain all this to Viktor."

"I found a spot for a picnic not far down the mountain and not visible from the fort." Zen nodded to the beginnings of a trail.

Of course, she had. It was almost as if her hospitality gene couldn't help but kick in. Not that Bri was complaining. She was tired, thirsty, and starving and if Zen wanted to perform miracles and produce food and water and perfect picnic spots, she was certainly all for it.

Bri

ZEN LED THE way down a surprisingly easy trail that relaxed the steep grade with gentle switchbacks—an indication that generations of Marquardtians walked or rode horses everywhere. Bri and the others shot the scenery and chattered into their cameras as if this were a part of the sanctioned tour. They followed the trail into a line of trees that snaked across a flat patch of the mountain. The coolness from the canopy of leaves felt good.

Bri heard water up ahead. Of course, it made sense for the trees to grow near a constant source of water.

"There's a place next to the stream," Zen said as they rounded a large tree. "It looks like a popular spot for the locals to hang out."

The trickling sound from the rocky stream cast a calm soothing blanket over a clearing bordered by propped up rough logs, creating long benches facing a circle of ashes.

"Wow." Sally walked to the edge of the water. "I bet it's cold."

"Freezing." Zen pulled a water filter from her backpack. "In case you want to refill your bottles after lunch."

Bri joined the others on the logs, opened her bag, and took out a water bottle— a sleek durable burgundy bottle with the Double B logo. And there were two of them in the bag. Subtle marketing at its best. Something that seemed to be missing in Marquardt.

Zen sat next to Bri and opened her bag.

"I take it your family owns this resort?" Bri held up the bottle.

Zen nodded as she unwrapped what looked like a ciabatta roll filled with vegetables and cheese. "It's one of my family's oldest properties, over a hundred years old."

"And it'll benefit from Marquardt opening up," Joe said.

Mick raised his water bottle. "Would you rather stay at a hundred-year-old Italian resort or a modern glass monstrosity?"

"I'm afraid my family is gearing up to take full advantage of our properties surrounding Marquardt, including day trips to here." Zen shrugged. "My aunt much prefers to help prepare Marquardt for tourists, but . . ."

"Frankly, I don't see how this opening the border thing is going to happen. Great sandwich, by the way." George nodded at his overstuffed sandwich.

"You know what we need to do?" Kristy looked around at them. "We need to talk to the head honcho."

"Exactly." Joe leaned forward. "He has to see this country from our point of view. That's why we're here. Right?"

"In the meantime, we need to create our own adventures." Mick pointed his sandwich at Zen. "Like Zen's doing."

"I'd rather just walk," Zen said.

"Exactly." George put his sandwich onto the wrapper. "That's why we're all here. We each have a niche, an angle, and we need to show this country through our personal lens to our followers. If we're not allowed to do that, what's the point of us being here?"

"And tourists expect to do things spontaneously," Zen said. "I don't think Marquardt is ready for that at all."

Bri pulled a slim white paper sleeve from the bottom of the bag and peeked inside it. Two cookies.

"Cookies," Sally squealed. "Thank you."

Zen smiled. "The bakery caters to Americans and bakes chocolate chip cookies. They seemed the best choice of sweet."

"You know"—Mick pointed a cookie at Zen—"Marquardt pretty much shot itself in the foot not hiring your family. They would have gotten a century's worth of hospitality and be ready on day one."

"So, we need to get Viktor to let us have a sit down with the president," Joe said. "What's his name?"

"Birkhofer," Zen said.

"What do we know about him?" Joe asked.

"He's a young guy," George said. "Charismatic political type. Maybe more interested in being president than knowing how to do the job—"

"Or keep his campaign promises," Kristy said.

George nodded. "That's the main thing. Is he over his head or does he care that the country's not prepared?"

Zen ran her hands through her messy curls.

"Just spit it out," Mick said. "How bad can it be?"

Zen straightened. "My aunt got the impression that he's in over his head. He's not strong enough to stand up to his ministers, who seem to have grasped only the greedy capitalism of modern society."

"I'm guessing the ministers are all male and old enough to be his father," Kristy said.

"Yeah, something like that."

Bri flashed a curious look at Zen. Her usual confident calm seemed deflated.

"Well, maybe they just need a reality check," Joe said. "We need to meet with all of them."

Lunch over, everyone gathered their trash, stuffed it into their packs, and refilled their water bottles using Zen's filter.

"Thank you for the great lunch," Jon said. "How can we pay you for it?"

Looking uncomfortable, Zen held up her hands as she shook her head. Bri frowned, then it hit her. Zen was embarrassed about being rich. Bri tried to imagine growing up not wanting for anything in a world of penthouses and rolling estates, private schools, and being driven everywhere. But there was something more. Hospitality was literally in her blood. She was simply doing what came naturally to her—making sure everyone else was comfortable.

"How about dinner's on us," Mick said. Of course he got it, being from a well-to-do family himself.

Zen brightened. "Sounds like a deal."

"You'll just have to find a place to eat that's not trying to harden our arteries," Mick added.

They all laughed and relaxed as they followed Zen downstream to a line of stones that crossed the gurgling water. Stones of different sizes and questionable stability. Zen walked across them like it was a sidewalk. Bri surprised herself by being the next across and receiving a sparkling grin from Zen.

"Having fun?" Zen asked as the others crossed the stream.

Bri blinked at her. She *was* having fun. Here. Way out of her comfort zone, with people who were both competitors and peers. "Yeah, I am."

"Good."

Kristy squawked as she almost lost her balance in the middle of the stream.

"You always seem a little uncomfortable when you're in nature." Zen shook her head at Jon taking two stones at a time.

Bri stared at Zen. Had she been projecting her ambivalence toward nature somehow? "You can tell?"

"It's not an overt thing," Zen said. "Just that you seem more comfortable in towns."

Bri pushed down her rising panic. The last thing she needed was to project any kind of not-wanting-to-be-there vibe in her vlogs.

"Nature's especially nice with the right company." Zen flashed a grin as she turned to lead the way.

Bri stared after her as the others tromped past. Was she talking about her?

Zen

ZEN FELT AN odd disappointment as they followed the last gentle switchback, and the trail neatly deposited them on the gravel and dirt road she had discovered earlier that day. She could have spent all day leisurely walking next to Bri.

She even enjoyed listening to her fellow travelers chattering away to their cameras and to each other. The best part, Bri seemed more interested in walking than shooting and talking. Zen found herself strolling beside her in what she would call a companionable silence. Bri's presence seemed to be a conversation in itself, punctuated by their occasional glances and smiles at each other.

They spread out across the road as they rounded a small bend and saw the van up ahead, where the gravel met the paved road. Viktor was standing in the middle of the gravel road with crossed arms and confrontational body language.

"He doesn't look very happy," Mick said with a grin.

Zen glanced around and everyone looked game for whatever they were literally walking into. They had their cameras aimed at Viktor as they approached. Whatever happened, there would be plenty of photographic evidence.

They stopped about ten feet away from Viktor. Close enough to see his scowl and attempt at looking tough.

"Enjoy your walk?" Viktor asked in a way that suggested he didn't think they enjoyed it at all.

"Yes," Kristy said. "It was wonderful. This is a beautiful country."

Viktor stared at her startled and then looked at all of them. "Let's get the women on the van to rest, so us men can have a conversation."

Zen glanced at Bri, who looked ready to burst.

"You must be exhausted from standing here waiting for us," Bri said. "Why don't you rest in the van, and we'll continue our pleasant walk to the town?"

Bri looked surprised at herself for being so bold, and Zen couldn't stop her delighted grin.

Viktor's loss-for-words expression had taken on its own loss-for-words expression.

"Okay"—George stepped forward—"before you melt down into an existential crisis, we have a plan to help you deal with us."

Viktor riveted his attention on George.

"We, and I mean all of us, want to speak with President Birkhofer."

Viktor frowned and shook his head. "He is a busy man. Very busy busy."

"Busy with getting this border open." George put his hands behind his back and strolled a little closer to Viktor. Zen could picture him walking up an aisle in a classroom as he focused on a student who wasn't quite grasping a concept. "He has to talk to us because only we can help him."

"It is not that simple," Viktor said. "There are committees and ministers involved. Everything must be approved by the government council."

George performed a theatrical shrug. "Then I guess our visit here isn't worth your time or ours."

Viktor's eyes widened with panic. "Wait, wait. We are ready. We have many, many attractions ready for tourists."

Joe stepped forward. "Attractions are only a part of why people visit a place. The most important reason is the people. You've done some work on preparing the country physically, but you haven't prepared the people mentally. If you don't fix that, this venture will fail."

Viktor opened his mouth and then closed it.

"Do you want to be the one to explain our behavior to your boss?" Mick asked.

Viktor blinked at him.

"Look, Viktor," George said. "We know you're caught between a rock and a hard place. We like you. We don't want to see you get into trouble because of us."

Viktor opened his mouth and almost said something this time.

George clasped his hands together. "So, it's agreed. We pay a visit to your president. We'll be sure to tell him that you're doing your job with great diligence and professionalism."

The wheels in Viktor's head were creaky but definitely turning. He slowly nodded. "I take you to hotel for lunch and arrange a meeting with President Birkhofer this afternoon." He looked as if he was struggling with something. "For all of you."

Zen and the travelers grinned and exchanged high-fives. They still may decide to leave Marquardt but, at least, they'll have a great story to tell. And Aunt Fiona will be pleased that the opportunity she could only wish for was going to happen.

6
Day Two — Afternoon
Bri

THE RESTAURANT TURNED out to be a good hang out place. The staff, all young people, seemed to be more tolerant of unrelated women and men around a table together. Best of all, they could indulge in their caffeinated beverage of choice while they waited for an audience with the president.

"Not what I expected to be doing here." Kristy sipped her coffee and sighed. "If nothing else, we need them to get in a machine that makes lattes."

Zen stirred sugar and cream into a fresh cup of tea. She seemed somehow detached, pre-occupied with something. Something that had removed the twinkle from her eyes. Of course, Bri was dying to know what it was.

"Who's going to take the lead in the thing?" Joe asked.

They all looked around the table. Zen was still focused on her tea.

"The logical choice is Zen, since she understands all of this stuff," Sally said.

Zen blinked up. "George is the best choice because the president is used to listening to older men."

George straightened. "I have no problem with doing the basic stuff, but I'd appreciate backup with the niggling details."

Zen sipped her tea and shrugged.

"Come on, Zen." Jon, already too high energy, was practically levitating from all the Coke he'd been drinking like water. Thank god they didn't have energy drinks, or he'd be combusting. "This country needs to join the rest of the world. And we have the opportunity to make it happen. How amazing is that?"

Zen getting up and walking away popped into Bri's head. She realized Zen didn't like conflict. Bri was glad she hadn't mentioned how she felt about being in direct competition with her for followers.

Rapid footfalls echoed in the empty dining room, and Bri and the others turned to the entrance. Viktor was weaving around the tables to them in an awkward trot.

He glanced behind him and then put on his happy tour guide face. "Good news. That special event is ready. Just follow me."

They gathered their camera equipment and slurped down last sips of their drinks. Bri's nerves revved up to eleven as she stood. She felt a gentle hand under her elbow. Zen was somehow there as if sensing her unsteadiness.

"He's the president of a postage stamp not big enough to lick," she said in a low voice.

Bri glanced at her and was happy to see the twinkle back in her eyes.

They followed Viktor across the deserted lobby to a double door. He opened one of the doors and motioned them to enter. Bri looked around surprised. She wasn't expecting a small theatre with cushy seats—like the private movie theaters in rich people's homes. She glanced at Zen. She probably lived in places with this kind of theater. Maybe still did. Bri had no idea where Zen called home.

Sally went to the second row and plopped down in a seat. "Kind of bougie for a convention hotel."

They spread out over the twenty or so seats. Bri looked at the double doors and realized Viktor had stayed outside. To guard the door maybe?

"Kind of small for movie night," Mick said.

They waited in silence, watching the door on the side of the stage opposite the double doors. All except Zen, who seemed to be lost in her thoughts again.

They heard a noise on the other side of that door, and it opened inward. A young man probably in his thirties, sporting a neatly trimmed tuff of blond hair, walked in. He was wearing a sweater and casual slacks and carrying a baseball cap. He looked the travelers over with a kind of sheepish expression, his face almost boyish. Bri could see how a country that had lived for years under an aging dictator would find this charismatic, engaging young man the perfect choice for leading them into the twenty-first century. And yes, even without saying a word or doing anything but stand there, his charisma wafted off of him like a strong perfume.

The man looked up at them and smiled. "I'm Gustav Birkhofer. It's so good to see you all in person. I feel as if I already know you through your vlogs." He held up his hands. "Before you say anything, I have to admit, I'm glad you asked for this meeting."

Bri exchanged glances with the other travelers. Not only for his words but for his nearly accent-less English.

"You don't have to tell me about the problems you're facing." He sat on a folding chair that Viktor must have placed there for him. "I know we're not ready."

"Viktor hinted that your ministers have strong opinions about all this," Joe said.

Birkhofer looked up with a bitter laugh. "That's the very polite way of putting it."

"So, what can we do to help you?" George asked.

Birkhofer shook his head, looking despondent. "I don't know if anything can be done. The ministers only see the piles of money flowing around Marquardt like water around a boulder. And they want that money to pour through here. They think that a hotel like this one and fast food and brand name stores are enough to lure tourists here to spend their money."

"Who put that weird idea into their heads?" Mick asked.

Zen, a few seats down from Bri, shifted. Of course, she knew.

"An American businessman named Henry Fitz." Birkhofer sighed. "He told them exactly what they wanted to hear so they contracted the modernization with him. The ministers wouldn't listen when I tried to explain that Fitz was only interested in making—to use an American expression—a quick buck off of us and didn't care at all about how we were going to get tourists without making some major changes in our culture."

Bri glanced at Zen. Something close to anger flashed in her eyes.

"This hotel is an unfortunate misstep that can be overlooked if visitors are allowed to freely experience your country," George said. "To walk the trails, to visit the businesses in the town, to eat in the restaurants, to go to your cultural and historical attractions and be greeted by locals happy to see all of us. Trained in hospitality." He looked around. "We can try to convince the ministers that opening the border is going to fail. That's why we're here, after all. To be the test run for you."

Birkhofer shifted on the chair. "Uh, bringing you here was my idea, and the ministers only saw the free publicity from it. They thought, you stay in the hotel, we take you to all the sights, and you show what a great place it is." He emitted a rueful chuckle. "They're used to people simply following instructions without thought."

"I have a question," Sally said. "How did these ministers become ministers because it sounds like they're at odds with what you want to do."

Birkhofer gazed at the back of the auditorium and then turned his attention to Sally. "The type of government structure could not be decided on because no one was in charge after Krieger died. The only certainty was everyone wanted it to be a democratic government. So, they thought the first thing to do was to put someone in charge who would then have the authority to implement how the government is structured."

"I take it that's not how it happened," George said.

Birkhofer nodded. "There was one caveat. And the people voted on allowing this caveat when they voted for president. All the members of the interim government must have served in leadership positions in the previous regime and continue to serve for three more years to help in the transition to a democratic government."

Joe put his head in his hands, and George plopped back into the seat.

Birkhofer stood. "I'm sorry all of you have been dragged into this. I'll understand if you want to leave."

Bri exchanged alarmed looks with the others. Leave? She was ready to stay and set this country on the right track. But she had no idea how they could do that. Not with a wall of old regime ministers blocking progress.

Zen stood. "There are three ministers, right?"

Birkhofer nodded.

"Invite them to this little meeting."

Birkhofer stared at Zen as if she had sprouted an extra arm. "They don't know I'm meeting with you." He waved the baseball cap. "I sneaked out to get here."

"But you're their boss. Right?" Zen asked.

Birkhofer gazed at her for several moments. "Yes. Yes, I am."

"Tell them you've arranged an opportunity for them to meet with your test visitors who are very interested in talking to them," Zen said.

Bri and the others stared at her with both apprehension and great interest.

Zen shrugged. "The worse that can happen is they won't be happy that you ventured out without consulting them. Even though meeting with visitors is within the purview of a president."

"What are you going to do with them?" Birkhofer asked.

Zen's amused half-smile broke through her serious demeanor. "Give them a much-needed reality check."

Zen

FOR THE FIRST time since entering Marquardt, Zen felt a cautious optimism. She approached Birkhofer after he finished his phone call to summon the ministers.

"Hi, I'm Zen Benbrook," she said in a quiet voice.

Birkhofer's eyes widened as he grasped her hand with both of his and shook it. "I didn't know you were a Benbrook."

"I don't mention it anywhere on social media, but it's an open secret." Zen cocked her head. "Are you interested in some pointers?"

Birkhofer released her hands. "I'd be grateful for any help you can provide."

Zen nodded as she turned away from the curious eyes of other travelers.

Bri

VIKTOR KEPT GLANCING at them as he brought in three more chairs.

"Thank you, Viktor," Birkhofer said. "I'll let you know if we need anything else."

Viktor gave them one last uncertain look as he closed the door behind him.

"Whose side is Viktor on?" Kristy asked, staring at the door.

"He owns a dairy and volunteered to help with the transition early on," Birkhofer said. "He's an earnest and diligent worker and was the best candidate to be your handler that met the ministers' approval. He's enthusiastic about opening the borders and learned as much as we were allowed to teach him. My team and I spent a year going around the world absorbing everything. We prepared learning materials for classes aimed at the business owners and the rest of the citizens. We knew we would have an uphill battle on some issues, such as women's rights, but we gave ourselves six months for them to wrap their minds around it for the good of the country."

He glanced at the door. "The ministers insisted that they had to approve the materials and then removed all the things they didn't like, which was just about everything that needed to be done."

"Didn't they think not doing these things would keep tourists away?" Mick asked.

Birkhofer glanced at the door again and stepped closer to the seats. The travelers leaned in. "You have to understand, they truly think tourists will follow any rules imposed on them and still enjoy their visit."

The door opened and three men walked in looking around with annoyed and curious expressions. They saw the travelers and their faces darkened in unison.

The one with slicked back grey hair and a beer gut that barely held in an expensive-looking blue suit barked something in guttural German.

"He's upset about us females," Zen said.

All three men glared at her. So, they understood English.

The stocky man with salt-and-pepper bushy eyebrows and no hair, also in an expensive-looking suit glared at her. "You do not have permission to speak. Which one of these men is your husband?"

The third man was thin and probably north of eighty. His brown suit was nicely tailored but not as ostentatious as the other men's. He eyed the travelers with a wary scowl. Altogether a nice friendly group.

Zen rose to her feet. "First off, I have no husband. Second off, I've brokered deals twenty times the worth of your country to help make places successful tourist destinations. Even though I'm not directly in that business anymore, I'm close enough that I can't avoid hearing things. Like, for instance, you paid Henry Fitz two-and-a-half times more than all he's done here is worth, plus you gave him free reign over everything. An interesting strategy, carelessly draining the country's coffers to make money."

The three men straightened, outrage sparking in their eyes.

"What do you know?" The stocky man shook his fist at her. "You're just a woman. You don't know anything about doing business."

"There are plenty of men you can ask, who will tell you the same thing," Zen said, unruffled. "I'll give you their names."

The men stopped their posturing and stared at her.

Bri and the other travelers looked at each other. These despicable men knew they had been bamboozled by Fitz. She wondered how much of that overpayment ended up in the ministers' own pockets.

Birkhofer turned to them, looking shocked. "What? You said everything's too expensive, and we not only got a good deal, we came in under budget."

The men glanced at the travelers as they babbled in German with imploring hands. Zen looked amused. Bri couldn't wait to ask her later what they were saying.

"Enough," Birkhofer finally said. He straightened and faced the men. "Have a seat, gentlemen."

The ministers shot impatient looks at him but sat on the chairs on the stage.

"We're marketing ourselves as a budget-friendly, affordable Alpine experience." Birkhofer put his hands behind his back and casually walked around the ministers. "On the day we start selling our tourist packages, the resorts, lodges, hotels, towns throughout the Alpine region are ready to offer cheaper packages." He stopped in front of them and took in their shocked expressions. "A rookie mistake of announcing our intentions before implementing them. And your reaction will be, we'll just announce a special first-to-experience-Marquardt discount and offer packages at even a lower price. And we'll be in the hole before we're able to afford the rope to pull ourselves out."

The man in the blue suit shook a finger at Birkhofer. "You don't know what you're talking about. How do you know what the other resorts will do?"

Birkhofer produced a sly grin. "Because it's my job to know."

The ministers' expressions darkened and the oldest opened his mouth to speak. Birkhofer slashed a finger at him, and he shut his mouth, looking surprised at Birkhofer showing an actual backbone.

"Don't get me wrong," Birkhofer said. "The others don't want to see Marquardt fail. In fact, they're delighted we're finally opening our borders and allowing foreigners to come and go."

"Ha." The stocky minister waved a hand in disdain. "That's nonsense."

Birkhofer gave him an indulgent smile. "And that's why I'm president and you're not. I have a better understanding of these things."

The stocky minister glared at him. He must have been the opponent who lost by a humiliating landslide.

Bri turned to Zen. Her pleased expression told Bri all she needed to know about how Birkhofer was doing.

"While it's true everyone is in competition for the same tourist money, there is also a symbiotic relationship between businesses and even countries." Birkhofer sat in the front row, looking both relaxed and in charge. "For instance, Marquardt's infrastructure is limited for vehicle traffic, but it's perfect for people interested in hiking, cross-country skiing, mountain biking. Both Italy and Austria have a series of trails that have to go around Marquardt. Hooking up with these systems will create a great business for the farms as rest stations and hostels."

"Riffraff stomping around our country," the old man spat out.

Birkhofer gazed at him. "They're regular tourists with just as much money and probably more than the type of tourist you'd attract with your budget rate. But you know this already, since you've seen our research. My team and I concluded that joining the trail system and putting in small eateries, rest places, and hostels are an excellent way to attract tourists. And offering workshops for our crafts, such as making cow bells, learning how to play the alphorn, cheesemaking, weaving . . . It's all in our master plan. The plan you rejected."

"How much money will that bring in?" the man in the blue coat asked with a sneer.

"Actually," Birkhofer said, "more than this hotel. I'm sure the numbers Fitz gave you were based on a one hundred percent occupancy every single day of the year. The average occupancy of hotels in Europe is sixty-three percent. Factoring in the budget price, the cultural misogyny you want to maintain, and the general distrust of visitors our citizens are displaying, I'd say the type of tourist we'll attract are senior citizens who want everything done for them, extreme religious and philosophical sects who agree with your views toward women, and men who will figure out how to use Marquardt for shady purposes."

Holy cow. Bri exchanged amazed looks with the others. Zen had certainly fed Birkhofer a lot of good information.

"We have two very different plans for tourist development," Birkhofer said. "Since this involves the welfare of everyone in Marquardt, the democratic thing to do is to present our plans to the people and let them vote for the one they think will be best for the country. Presentation, of course, means including all research and statistics to back up your plan. Keeping in mind that that the plans with the most details on how they will directly help the people usually gets the most votes . . ."

The ministers exchanged hardened glances.

The oldest one stood and stepped forward. "Your plans will ruin Marquardt."

Birkhofer held up a finger. "Correction. My plans will stop your pockets from being lined by the likes of Fitz."

The ministers sputtered but could only glare at him.

"You told the people that going with Fitz was the cheapest, most cost-efficient way to get Marquardt ready for tourists." Birkhofer pushed himself out of the seat and put himself right in front of the ministers. "Within the hour, I'm releasing to the people the estimate from Benbrook, and the payments and ongoing expenses to Fitz."

The ministers clambered to their feet. "You wouldn't dare."

Birkhofer waggled his hand. "I won't under one condition."

"What?" The man in the blue suit looked ready to explode.

"You have to agree to the condition, in writing, before I tell you what it is."

Bri glanced at Zen. She was grinning in delight. Bri had the feeling that it was one of Zen's own tricks back in the day.

The ministers did more sputtering and protesting.

Birkhofer turned to the travelers and gave them a gracious bow of the head. "Thank you for your feedback on whether we're ready to open the border yet. I think the ministers and I have some paperwork to attend to."

Zen

ZEN STOOD AT the picture window in the non-descript third floor conference room in the ministry building, gazing at the snow glistening on a peak just a few miles away and culturally on another planet. She was there to do a job she had happily and almost literally walked away from eight years earlier.

Sorry, Aunt. This wasn't invoking fond memories of what to her had been a soulless job. She wasn't the type to get satisfaction from moving in for the kill and winning. She could only feel the satisfaction of not losing.

Fiona not only wanted her back to do her old job, she wanted her to climb the corporate ladder, to be groomed to take over the company one day. Simply because Fiona thought she had seen her own self in Zen, when Zen started working for the company at sixteen. Fiona herself had been on the lower rungs of the company ladder at that time, but had been smart enough to grab onto Zen and pull her up behind her.

The doors opened, and she turned as a grinning Birkhofer entered with several other people, including women. They were all young, exuded enthusiasm and competence, and dressed in modern business casual. They wouldn't be out of place at a trendy startup.

"Thank you for waiting. Please sit." Birkhofer pointed to the chair at the end of the conference table.

Zen took a seat, while the others, looking ready to burst with excitement, slipped into chairs around the table with Birkhofer at the other end.

"This is my team," Birkhofer said. "My real team. As you can see, women have been a part of my transition from the beginning."

"I'm happy to hear that," Zen said.

The grinning woman adjacent to Zen pushed a thick stack of papers to her. "We're all so happy to meet you. We had no idea Zen Traveler was the amazing Zen Benbrook."

Zen stared at her, having no idea how to respond. "Uh, happy to be able to help."

"Ms. Fiona Benbrook has made some very generous amendments to the original proposal to help us recover from the financial hole Fitz has put us in," Birkhofer said. "We are also beginning the process of recovering the kickbacks Fitz has made to the ministers and others. We can't begin to thank you for everything."

Zen took in the earnest faces of this group, who were no doubt on their way to taking Marquardt into a promising future, as they gazed at her as if she and Benbrook were their savior. "I will let my aunt know her investment in Marquardt is much appreciated and I foresee a strong and healthy relationship between us for years to come."

Birkhofer held up two fountain pens. "Let's get these papers signed then, so your company can get to work."

7
Day Three
Bri

THAT ONE CONDITION was, the ministers and everyone who were profiting from Fitz's involvement in Marquardt, plus those people in government still loyal to the old regime, were required to resign by end of yesterday. If they didn't resign, they'd be escorted to the border and exiled forever. Not only that, Birkhofer ordered an audit of everything Fitz did, checking building materials, checking construction, third-partly vendors, auditing all the finances . . . Zen said her aunt was more than happy to mentor Birkhofer on how to sue Fitz into the dark ages.

Now they had no more Viktor. No more restrictions on their movements. They were free to do what they wanted, or were they? Really. People weren't going to change their minds literally overnight.

Bri did an extra careful job of putting all her camera equipment into her backpack. Everything was charged and all the memory cards were cleared and ready. She wanted to have the best vlog coming from this first day of navigating Marquardt on her own.

Except. She didn't know what to do. Birkhofer had emailed them a list of what Marquardt had to offer, plus a rather sketchy map. But how did they get there? Were the locals actually expecting visitors? At least they didn't have to worry about the money situation. The one thing Birkhofer did get implemented was a way for all the businesses to take credit cards. Of course, the ministers had agreed to anything where the money flowed into the country, including receiving permission to use Euros from the Council of the European Union. Zen had explained how all that worked when the whole gang had commandeered a couple of tables at Frau Mueller's last night.

Bri turned to Zen, who was sitting cross-legged in front of the sliding glass door. She couldn't tell if Zen was deep into meditation or just looking outside. Zen's natural state seemed to be half-meditating.

Zen glanced back as if she had heard Bri's thoughts. Kind of spooky actually.

"Beautiful day," she said.

Bri walked to the window and gazed outside. It *was* a beautiful day. The striking snowy mountains rose up beyond the valley, too huge and imposing to be real. Too bad they were in Austria or Italy, she really didn't know which direction the countries were, since they both kind of wrapped around Marquardt.

"I suppose you're going to walk the border perimeter or something—before lunch." Bri tried to sound casual, not desperately hoping Zen invited her along on wherever she was going. Or at least until they ran into the other travelers.

Zen flashed her an amused look. "Not this trip. We're here to show our followers why they should come to Marquardt, so I thought to start in the town proper today."

"Visiting shops and things? That's more my style," Bri said.

Zen smiled at the small birds pecking at something on the sidewalk. "I hope you don't mind me tagging along then. So, you can take the lead on this part of the adventure."

What . . . ? Bri stared down at Zen, who continued to watch the birds. "Uh, sure." She mustered a smile and realized she didn't have to muster too much. "It'll be fun."

Zen gracefully rose to her feet. "It'll be a different experience, I think."

"At least you know the language." Bri returned to her backpack to make sure she had everything.

"Yeah." Zen chuckled as she buckled on her camera belt and slipped on her backpack. "I don't think the rudimentary English they had to learn is adequate for when they feel the need to voice their opinions about us loose foreigners. And it'll probably blow up our phone translators."

Bri settled her backpack onto her shoulders and turned to Zen. "How much trouble do you think we'll have with the locals?"

Zen cocked her head. "I think the younger generation will surprise us."

Bri laughed. "No surprise there. They want what all young people in the world want."

"And they have the added bonus of the government actually sanctioning their rebellion against their elders."

"So, there's hope for Marquardt?" Bri asked as she opened the door.

Zen stopped. "There's always hope. We just have to find the right path to get to it."

Bri

THE TOWN LOOKED different in the daytime. Bri hadn't realized the cobblestone road to the restaurant was the only way into the walled part of the city, at least on the hotel side. She shot some footage of the narrow lane that split around a small green area up toward what looked a central section of town. The two- and three-story timber-framed buildings curved with the lane, the timber balconies leaning over it in places. The stone they walked on was cut in different shapes and paved in intricate patterns. Beautiful and something she'd never seen before.

Bri pointed the camera at herself as they walked down the middle of the lane and voiced these simple observations. Zen turned and gave a beaming thumbs up. *Yeah. Why did I think this was so hard?*

Bri tried to discern shops from offices to whatever was behind these walls of different sizes but all built with the same timber and white facades. The town looked as if it had been scrubbed down to the grout but sparkled cold, instead of inviting. None seemed to have the typical trappings used to lure in tourists. The only locals were women in drab skirts and heavy shoes, carrying large bags made out of sturdy material. The few men were pushing what looked like wares on delivery carts to the shops.

"Grocery shopping is an everyday thing," Zen said. "No supermarkets or infrastructure for food with a long shelf life."

"Sounds healthier," Bri said.

"Except when you can't get fruits and vegetables in the winter."

They stepped onto the grass of the park that seemed to be the center of town. Several lanes, some no wider than a path, spoked out from the park and wound out of sight up and down the hills. They stopped in front of a pedestal with no statue on it and studied each potential way to go.

Zen cocked her head at Bri. "Eeny, meeny, miny, moe?"

Before Bri had a chance to decide how to decide, a patter of feet came from the widest lane.

"Hey, there they are." A grinning Jon trotted to them, followed by a walking Mick, Sally, and Kristy. "We can't make heads or tails of this place." He planted himself in front of Bri and Zen, barely able to contain his excess exuberance. "First off, it's a maze with dead ends. Maps are definitely a must. Second, they invite us here to test their tourist-readiness and there aren't any shops doing any touristy things."

"Yeah." Kristy plopped down on a concrete bench. "I'm afraid to walk into what looks like a general store. We've been getting enough glares from the women out shopping."

Zen paced a circle around the little park, studying the grass. She looked as if she was thinking, so Bri and the others just watched her and hoped she came up with something good. She finally looked up, surprised that their attention was on her.

"Let's visit the bakery," she said.

Mick pointed to the lane they had just come from. "It's down here. The aromas from it are amazing. It was the closest I got to going into a place."

They found their own space as they walked down the lane and talked to their cameras about how the first shop they were visiting was the bakery with the heavenly aromas, which were wafting to Bri like a scented echo in the narrow canyon formed by the looming buildings. All of them except Zen, who didn't do much talking and walking. She usually shot as she walked and noted where she was when she got there. The viewer simply enjoyed the sights and sounds of the journey with her. Bri kind of envied her ability to create videos that were both calming and engaging in a minimalist way.

They walked up to a shop with yellow, instead of bright white panels between the deep brown timber frames. A wooden shingle with a colorful rendition of a loaf of bread painted on it hung over a door that looked as old as the building. The oversized window not only displayed loaves of rustic bread but surprisingly colorful pastries. Surprising because they were the most festive and, for lack of a better word, frivolous thing Bri had seen so far in Marquardt.

"Have your Google translators ready," Zen said. "Helps to get an immediate lay of the land so to speak."

"What happens if they're hostile to us?" Sally asked.

"We practice winning them over to the idea that we're what they will be facing when the tourists come to town."

Mick rubbed his cheek with an amused look. "Why do I think that's not as easy as it sounds."

Zen laughed as she pulled open the door. The aroma that had been driving Bri crazy crashed into her senses. One of everything, please.

The shop was a study in white, bright, and clean, like the town but a hundred times more inviting. Bri felt as if she was stepping into another world from the cold, unfriendly one outside. A stainless-steel counter and glass display cases ran the length of the narrow store with a standing counter on the opposite wall. She raised her camera to shoot the scene. She'd add a voiceover later.

A young woman in what looked like a baggy white T-shirt and tightly wrapped white apron watched them with wide-eyed fascination from behind the counter.

Zen walked up to the counter and smiled at her. "Guten Morgen. English?"

The young woman straightened. "Yes." She lifted her finger for a second and then smiled. "How . . . may I . . . help . . . you?"

Zen grinned. "Sehr gut."

The young woman looked ready to burst from smiling.

"I'm Zen." Zen held out her hand over the counter.

"Lisle." The young woman shook Zen's hand. "How may I help you?" She grinned, looking pleased with herself.

Sally stepped up to the counter and pointed to a chocolate-covered something or other. "What is this?"

She held her phone up and a digital voice asked the question in German. Lisle's eyes widened as she stared at the phone.

Lisle answered in excited German. Sally looked at the English translation. "Chocolate covered pastry with vanilla cream inside."

"Sounds good," Mick said from where he was studying the pastries further down the counter.

Bri watched as the others asked questions, showed Lisle how the phone translator worked, and helped her with using the tablet-based credit card terminal.

She saddled up to Zen, who was shooting the scene. Zen lowered her camera and gave Bri her attention.

"How did you know this place would be friendly?" Bri asked.

Zen shrugged but couldn't keep the twinkle from her eyes. "I walked past here yesterday on the way to the government building. The door stood open, and I overheard a conversation between Lisle and a woman, most likely her mother. Her mother didn't think she could face us tourists but finally found a way her rebellious daughter could make herself useful."

"You said, look for the young people." Bri nodded as Lisle drank in everything the others were telling her. She wanted to know where they got their clothing, if they had cars and houses. If Sally and Kristy were allowed to drive . . .

"I have no doubt she's going to get together with her friends and tell them about us," Zen said. "And they're going to volunteer to run the shops or find a way to talk to us. The young people will save this country from plunging into another oligarchy."

Bri bought what Google told her was a Krapfen, which looked like a jelly-filled donut, and they finally stepped out of the shop. They looked around for Zen, then saw her through the window. Zen was still in the bakery giving something to Lisle. Lisle nodded, looking grateful and relieved for some reason.

"What was that about?" Mick asked as Zen joined them.

"I gave her about the equivalent of what she sold to us, so her mother won't accuse her of giving the pastries away," Zen said.

Jon's shocked expression was almost comical. "Why would she think that?"

"Because it's only numbers on a digital tablet and a paper receipt. The mother isn't going to trust credit cards until they receive the actual cash for the sales. And even then, it may take a long time."

"Maybe we should tell our followers to use cash as much as possible when they visit, at least until they get used to credit cards." Bri pulled out her notebook and jotted down the reminder.

Sally nodded. "Good idea."

"Looks like we owe you another dinner," Mick said to Zen.

Zen gave a half nod. "Frau Mueller is going to get sick of seeing us."

"Let the cheese burn and be scraped." Mick grinned as they trudged back to the park.

Bri squinted at a steeple peeking up from the buildings backdropped by the little mountain with the fort at the top. "Is that a church?"

Jon nodded enthusiastically. "It's one of the few things marked on the map the prez gave us. Originally built in the tenth century on top of a hill, surrounded by fields with the town clustered over there." He pointed to where they had entered through the wall.

They followed the most likely lane to a set of steps that emptied onto a cobblestone courtyard in front of a miniature Gothic-style church built out of rough white stone and a single spire rising from its roof.

George and Joe were standing in the open doorway and looking as if they were comparing notes.

"I should have known this is where'd you guys go." Mick laughed as everyone tromped across the courtyard.

George and Joe looked up.

"Well worth it. A little gem of a church." Joe spotted the pastry Kristy was nibbling. "Whoa. Where'd you get that?"

"A great bakery, straight that way on the other side of the park." Kristy pointed. "The girl, Lisle, is friendly and curious, so be prepared to answer lots of questions."

"Also, if you have Euros, use those instead of plastic," Mick said. "Zen says the oldsters won't trust credit cards until they actually see the money they made from them."

George nodded, thoughtfully. "That makes sense."

Bri and the others visited the church and spent the rest of the day wandering the maze of Marquardt City proper. They even ventured into a couple more shops where young people were working and were as enthusiastic as Lisle. Adding in all the time it took to set up and record the shots, and so on, the day went by quickly.

Bri was grateful for Zen's quiet coaching on what to shoot and how to get good footage. Zen had a way of asking for Bri's input on angles or views and their discussion led Bri to making a better shot than she would have on her own. Zen only seemed do it when she sensed Bri was about to miss an important shot and acted as if she was enjoying discovering the place with her. And maybe she was. Bri was still balancing how she had perceived Zen to be and how she seemed to be. Either way, Zen wasn't anything like Bri had expected her to be in real life.

Zen

ZEN STROLLED BEHIND the others as they almost bounced down the cobblestones toward Frau Mueller's. Their high spirits seemed to roll off them to the surrounding buildings that were glowing in the low afternoon sun.

Zen struggled to keep her giddiness from bursting through. Bri's inexperience in finding the best shots gave Zen the chance to casually interact with her while helping her. And it was fun. It had been a long time since Zen had hung out with someone because she enjoyed the company.

Zen grinned as Bri stopped and focused her camera on a window with rows of beer steins on display. Bri glanced at her, and Zen gave an encouraging nod while trying to make it look casual. Just being a friend supporting a friend.

Yeah, right.

She felt her phone buzz, pulled it out of her pocket, and inhaled a bracing breath. She put it to her ear. "Hi."

"If you actually worked for me you'd be getting a major promotion to chief miracle worker," Aunt Fiona said.

Zen rolled her eyes. "You were right about Birkhofer. He was on the right track, he was just hindered by the old regime's chain wrapped around his neck. As you've always said, find the weakest link in the chain and snap it."

"And you were the best chain snapper we've ever had."

Zen rolled her eyes again. "Present company, excluded."

"Hmm." Zen could picture Fiona's thoughtful expression. "The irony is, I was good but didn't have that one thing that made you really good."

Zen frowned. "What?"

"After figuring out that weak link, you had the ability to be the calmest person in the room and empower the right people," Fiona said. "You're the quiet, steady chess player, always several moves ahead and I was the in-your-face confrontational type. Both got the desired results, but your way didn't leave any lingering aftertaste. That's why I sent you to do the toughest negotiations."

"Yeah, I know," Zen said, softly.

"In hindsight," Fiona continued, "I realize how that wasn't the right way to nurture you and keep you in the company. It took me a long time to understand that you aren't a younger version of me."

"I wish I could have been." Zen stopped a couple of shops down from Frau Mueller's and waved at the others to go inside.

"You know, I've not given up on you, yet." Zen could hear the amusement in Fiona's voice. "You still have what it takes to lead a company."

Zen chuckled. "I'd not only keep everyone on their toes, but on their feet, following me around everywhere."

Fiona laughed. "Well, this little job for us will look great on your resume, whenever I think about retiring."

"My walking career is safe for a good long while then," Zen said.

Bri

BRI AND THE others plopped down on facing sofas and chairs in the empty hotel lobby after a leisurely meal at Frau Mueller's. She was feeling cautiously positive about this strange little country.

"I have to admit, I would have never predicted we'd have a fun day today." Sally sank into the sofa, looking as tired as Bri felt. "But I had fun."

"Very spontaneous," Jon said. "The best part of traveling."

Bri frowned at him. "Being spontaneous?"

"Oh, yeah." He nodded with his usual exuberance. "That's always when the magic happens."

"Magic?" Bri couldn't keep the skepticism from her voice. Today had been the most spontaneous day ever for her vlog, but she didn't feel anything magical.

"The week's still young." Zen was slumped in the chair opposite Bri with her legs stretched out and crossed. She wore a Cheshire Cat grin.

"The ever-enigmatic Zen making vague declarations." Joe shrugged. "What else is new?"

Zen returned the shrug. "Sometimes the magic is a bit shy and needs coaxing out." She grazed Bri with her glance.

Bri frowned again. "What are you saying, exactly?"

"Just that the rest of this trip will be us doing spontaneous things, since nothing is arranged." Zen re-crossed her legs.

"Well, I'm happy we can explore at will," Mick said. "Those electric mountain bikes Birkhofer bought before the ministers figured out what he was up to will come in handy."

George nodded. "Brilliant solution for getting around on all the unpaved roads and trails."

Bri listened as the others discussed the different places on the map Birkhofer had given them that were only accessible by foot or bicycle, realizing she'd be facing another morning of having to figure out what to do. She glanced at Zen, who was lazily gazing at her. Zen winked with an amused half-smile. Bri squinted at her. Why did she keep doing that?

She frowned at what sounded like doors opening. Any noise in the deserted lobby—deserted hotel—was amplified. They all turned to the front doors. A group of young people—Bri recognized Lisle and the young woman from Frau Mueller's—took a few steps inside and stopped and stared at what probably looked to them like a wondrous modern building.

"Wonder where they got the clothes," Kristy said.

Bri was so used to young people being dressed like, well, young people, their jeans, t-shirts, and sneakers didn't even register. But now that she saw them . . .

Lisle spotted them and led the way. The other young people looked both excited and uncertain.

Joe jumped up, went to the closest chair, and pushed it toward the circle of travelers. The young people joined in without hesitation until all the chairs and sofas were close together and angled so everyone could see each other. The travelers all greeted them like they had been expected and were happy to see them.

Bri was happy to see them but was beyond exhausted and still had to get everything uploaded to Josh.

"Okay, first thing," Mick said, when everyone was seated. "Where did you get your clothes?" He held out his phone so they could hear it in German.

They looked at each other.

"I'll translate for you," Zen said. "Much more efficient that using the app."

They gave her relieved looks and then turned to Lisle.

Lisle burst into an excited explanation that included pointing out articles of clothing and nods from the others.

"It seems Birkhofer's team had offered to order modern clothes to anyone who wanted them," Zen said. "This was before the ministers were able to stop his plan of action. Of course, the young people jumped at the chance. Their parents weren't quite as enthusiastic for themselves or for their kids. But the kids work in the businesses that tourists will visit and so Birkhofer's team convinced the parents that it was important they present a modern look to the people they'll be selling to."

"If Birkhofer had been able to do what he wanted to do, Marquardt would have been ready for tourists," Sally said.

They all agreed, and a lively conversation ensued. Bri got a second wind and found herself paying attention. Zen *did* have a mesmerizing voice. Bri couldn't explain why, and voice training was a part of her journalism education. Maybe it was the accentless English that suggested she was from nowhere and everywhere. Or the timbre of her voice, which was almost as androgenous as her appearance, but still distinctly female. Whatever it was, her voice was one of the reasons Bri watched her vlogs. Yes, she admitted it. Her interest in Zen was not all about checking out what her closest rival was doing.

Every once in a while Zen glanced Bri's way with an enigmatic smile. Did she feel the rivalry too? She had to. People were constantly starting which-solo-traveler-do-you-like-best threads, and they were always the top two. That was why Mick called Zen her archrival. That was how the social media world saw them.

After an hour or so, the young people worried that they had been out too late. As they reluctantly left, the travelers promised they would continue to explain the world to them.

George pushed out of his chair. "I don't know about all of you, but this has been a long day, and work still needs to be done."

Oh. Right. Bri hoped she wouldn't fall asleep at the computer.

Zen

ZEN STOOD IN the parking lot, squinting into the deepening darkness at the road to the border. Marquardt was about to have its first foreign invasion. She chuckled at the idea. She could picture Aunt Fiona in the front open-topped vehicle, standing and pointing at the offending glass monstrosity behind Zen and yelling, "That thing first!"

A low rumble disturbed the still air. Marquardt was going to be a lot noisier when tourists started tromping around. Something else for the locals to get used to.

Lights flashing in the distance morphed into bobbing headlights. The rumbling grew into roaring truck engines as the convoy emerged from the dark at a good speed. Zen retreated to under the overhang to avoid playing dodge the truck in the dark.

One by one, huge burgundy and white trucks with the Double B logo splashed on the sides rolled into the parking lot and parked side by side in row after row. Barnun and Bailey had nothing on Fiona's fix-it army for both size and spectacle. Fiona was also the queen of efficiency and made sure everything was mapped out down to the number of t-shirts to buy in each size for each shop.

The door to the cab of the truck parked closest to Zen popped opened and Frederica, Fiona's younger sister, hopped out and stretched out her rangy frame.

"Heard you need a little work done here," she said as she strode up to Zen and pulled her into a hug. "I haven't seen you since you decided to walk halfway across the world." She held Zen at arm's length. "Don't look too worse for wear."

"You should see the graveyard of shoes," Zen said.

Frederica laughed and looked up. "My god. What a monstrosity."

"Fiona always said you could perform miracles." Zen turned and studied the hotel.

"She didn't include a demolition crew, so it'll be less a miracle and more of reducing the sticking-out-like-a-sore-thumb glare."

They turned at the sound of truck doors opening and burgundy-and-white clad workers gathering around their crew leaders. In a few minutes, the parking lot was alive with lights being erected, backs of trucks being opened and emptied, and people swarming everywhere.

"Hope the loos aren't locked," Frederica said.

"Every public loo is open, and I asked Birkhofer to have keycards for every room ready so you can just pick them up at the service counter."

"Excellent." Frederica nodded as she waved a man over to her. "We'll get the day crew to bed."

"The restaurant is also open twenty-four-seven," Zen said.

"We got facilities, beds, and food." Frederica grinned, the excitement for attacking this challenge glistening in her eyes. "Downright luxury compared to a lot of places we've gone into."

Zen performed a mock bow. "Welcome to Marquardt."

Bri

BRI FELT SOMETHING gently shaking her shoulder. She opened her eyes and stared at her computer with the screensaver's abstract colors dancing on the screen. She blinked to her side. Zen was standing there.

"What time is it?" Bri asked.

"About midnight." Zen carried her bag to her computer.

"You just getting in?"

Zen nodded as she turned on her computer, removed her camera belt, and sat down. "My aunt sent a ton of people and equipment and all kinds of stuff. I had to answer a million questions."

Bri performed a sitting stretch. "You think they can really make this country tourist ready in a few days?"

Zen waggled her hand. "They'll be able to make it tourist acceptable and spend the next couple of months making it tourist ready."

Something about all this sounded too good to be true. There had to be a catch. "Who's paying for all this? That American guy pretty much fleeced this place."

Zen turned her chair and faced Bri. "There are advantages to being a hundred-and-nine-year-old company. Benbrook has pretty much seen and done it all. They have a good idea of what's going to work and what isn't in a place, and they also know how to implement changes in a quick and efficient way." She gave a European half shrug. "But it's still expensive to take over and not only implement changes but fix the mistakes. My aunt has agreed to a long-term investment with Birkhofer, but payback will be based on a percentage of the profit, not a fixed amount each year to make it easier on Marquardt, and Benbrook has two years exclusive for day trips into Marquardt. Benbrook runs the main tourist concession in town and provides all the tourist stuff—T-shirts, trinkets, steins—all with the Marquardt branding. They also want to run the tourist hostels and wayside places on the walking trails for a year. Plus a few smaller things directly related to tourism."

Bri stared at Zen, surprised she actually answered her question and not just say, trade secret or something. She was also surprised because it all sounded like a reasonable deal for literally saving a country from certain poverty and another dictator taking over. "That's pretty detailed for something put together and agreed upon in less than a day."

Zen responded with a vibrant grin.

"Why are you grinning?"

"I like that you can see things so quickly. A lot of people *do* think that everything happens at a snap of the fingers." She cocked her head. "I admit, my aunt was extremely unhappy she didn't get the Marquardt contract and was very happy when she found out about this adventure and that I had been chosen to participate. She knew that Fitz had fleeced this country and used all mediocre off the shelf stuff and most likely paid kickbacks to the ministers and other members of the old guard. What she wasn't completely sure about was how deep the misogyny and the mistrust of modern society was with the general population. So, she had already worked out a plan based on what Fitz did and didn't do and modified it after I let her know about all the other stuff."

"She was waiting in the wings to swoop in for a rescue." Bri moved her mouse to double check she had finished everything before she had passed out. She had. Phew.

Zen laughed. "She was very unhappy—which is about as close to rage that a Benbrook gets. Her way of venting is to make contingency plans so she doesn't miss an opportunity twice. Speaking of . . ." She glanced around, looking oddly uncertain. Hesitant. "Tomorrow, the hotel and town will be a chaotic circus. Since you let me tag along in town today, would you like to join me to see what will be the most talked about attraction in Marquardt? Something that's marked but unlabeled on Birkhofer's map." She gave Bri a hopeful look. "I'll even give you the exclusive to introduce it to the world."

Bri could only stare at her. "I don't understand."

"I'm trying to convince you to get on one of those electric bikes and venture to the most beautiful spot in Marquardt." Zen sat back in her chair.

"Just us?" Bri was still confused.

Zen nodded. "Sure."

"But why let me have the exclusive for it?"

"I used to see this spot from the river road when I worked at the Benbrook Resort, and I always hoped to be able to visit it someday." Zen looked at her hands and then raised those gentle, sincere eyes. "I could have gone to it that first day and included it in my vlog, but it seems too special not to experience it with someone." She shrugged. "So, I thought I could help with your aversion to nature, and as an award for your bravery in facing the wilds of Marquardt, you could be the first to vlog about it."

Bri cocked her head. "You do a lot of strange thinking when you're out walking alone."

Zen laughed. "You have no idea."

Bri relaxed. She was starting to understand Zen's impulse to be generous was part her gentle nature and part what she liked about her family business—the hospitality. And, Bri had to admit, her curiosity was tweaked about this wondrous spot. She had nothing else to do tomorrow, and all of them had to make their own adventures in the strange country, so she really had no reason to turn down such a simple request.

"I happen to have my schedule open tomorrow." Bri couldn't keep away her smile.

Zen nodded, also smiling. "Then pencil me in for after breakfast."

8
Day Four — Morning
Bri

THE ELECTRIC BIKES, it turned out, had been stored in one of the ballrooms of the hotel. By the time Bri and Zen had breakfast and were ready for a morning out in nature, the Benbrook crew, a swarm of burgundy T-shirts and white jeans, had lined the thirty or so bikes outside the front door, away from their worker bee activity.

Bri couldn't remember the last time she'd ridden a bike, and she'd never been on an electric one.

Zen stood next to her with arms crossed, studying the line of bikes. "They can't be too hard to figure out."

"You've never ridden an electric bike?" Bri didn't know why she was surprised.

"Bikes aren't really my thing." Zen went to the closest bike.

They were all identical, so, at least, they didn't have to decide which one they liked the best. Zen put up the kickstand and pulled it away from the others. "We can practice in the part of the parking lot my family hasn't taken over."

Bri gave the parking lot closest to the doors an amused look. Trucks, vans, cars, equipment, furniture, boxes upon boxes were strewn all over the place.

"Your aunt must have been really sure this was going to happen," she said.

Zen laughed. "Yeah. She had Marquardt scoped out and transitioned on paper down to the square inch. She made sure all the stuff and a crew were on hand, close by, to get here at a moment's notice."

Bri watched a group of young men and women put boxes on what looked like miniature pickup trucks with flat fronts. Everyone scurrying around seemed to know what to do and what went where. She had the feeling Benbrook wasn't an organization for slackers.

"And what if this didn't happen?" Bri went to the next bike in the line and rolled it next to Zen.

Zen waggled her head. "I really don't know. My aunt has never not gotten her way in the end."

Bri looked at her amazed. "Really?"

"Yep." Zen straddled the bike, pulled up a little pamphlet hanging from the handlebar, and opened it. She then looked at the gears on the handlebar. "Okay. Simple enough."

They figured out throttle and pedal assist and not hitting any Benbrook workers as they practiced in the lot. Zen pulled up to the lot's entrance and looked back as she waited for Bri.

"Ready for an adventure?"

Bri took a deep breath and throttled the motor. "There's nothing else to do."

Zen laughed. "That's the spirit."

They pushed off and coasted down the small hill and then slowed as they passed the opening in the town wall. They stopped and watched as the Benbrook crews unloaded boxes from the little trucks, added stuff to the shop facades, balanced on ladders to replace street signs . . . As far as Bri knew, they had started working as soon as they pulled in last night, just as the travelers were going to their rooms. And the hotel hallway was suddenly alive with people that morning as the shift changed.

"Better them than me," Zen said as she put her feet on the pedals and glided away on the smooth blacktop.

Bri pushed off and caught up with her, the air just cool enough for her light jacket—refreshing. Maybe mornings were the best time to experience nature.

Zen stopped and launched not one, but two drones. They obediently rose up and one to the front of them and the other behind. Zen resumed peddling with Bri behind her. Bri checked the drones as they followed along with them.

She rode up next to Zen. "How do they do that?"

"Pre-programmed," Zen said. "They have what is called a follow me mode and a backward flying mode, so I can shoot coming and going at the same time."

"Amazing." Bri watched the little drone in front fly away as it kept pace with them.

"I have to keep an eye on the batteries," Zen said. "So, I put them up for short periods in different kinds of scenery."

"You don't mind that I'm in the shots?"

Zen gave her a surprised look. "Why should I mind?"

"Solo traveler and all that?" Bri said as they pedaled up a little hill.

Zen shrugged. "I let my subscribers know that I'll probably not be going completely solo or do much walking on this trip." She stopped at the top of the hill and brought in her drones.

By the time they got to the scene of the confrontation with Viktor two days earlier, Bri was riding the bike without any trouble. The electric assist was great on the hills and easy on the legs. Zen showed her how to mount her GoPro on the handlebars to get travel footage. She also showed her how to set up a camera and ride away from it and go back and get it. Before they got to the crossroads, they set up their cameras beyond it, so they could shoot their approach to it.

Bri studied the gravel and dirt road. It hadn't been that hard to walk on, but on a bike?

"These are mountain bikes," Zen said. "The fatter tires make it easier to ride on unpaved roads and trails."

Bri gave her a dubious look but got caught up in her happy expression. "Why are you so happy?"

Zen held out her arms and looked all around. "It's a beautiful day and the beautiful countryside is almost calling out to be explored. This is why I do what I do. I love exploring and wanting to know what's around the next bend or over the next hill."

Bri stared at her as what had always been obvious sank into her dense brain. Whatever Zen's motivation and agenda was for vlogging, it truly was not the same as for the rest of them.

Still grinning, Zen turned to the unpaved road and kicked the bike forward. As Bri watched her glide away, a second obvious thought walloped her truly dense brain. Zen wasn't walking. She was absolutely religious about showing walking as her only mode of travel. Even when she said she had to take transportation for safety or practical reasons—usually across places that couldn't be walked for whatever reason—she never actually showed herself using those other means.

Bri blinked out of her curious thoughts and rolled onto the gravel and dirt and cautiously pedaled. Not too bad. She pedaled faster with the electric assist kicking in and caught up with Zen, who had stopped to place a camera in the middle of the road.

Bri looked at the road up ahead. The perfect shot for them disappearing around a bend. Bri set up her camera next to Zen's and they pedaled away from them.

As soon as they were out of sight of the cameras they stopped.

"I'll get them." Zen flipped down her kick stand and jogged back around the bend before Bri even had a chance to say anything.

Bri smiled at the fact that Zen jogged and not simply turned around on the bike and rode back. Her natural state was truly on her feet. Then why was she riding instead of walking? Was she doing it for Bri's benefit? Not that Bri was complaining. She knew she'd never be able to walk to wherever they were going, but as fast as Zen walked and as slow as Bri biked, they could have easily traveled together. It was probably that hospitality thing—like the comfort of the guest always came first.

They continued on the road past the path to the fort. Bri knew they were climbing, but it was gradual, and the electric assist made it easy—no exertion at all. They laughed at the mooing cows with their huge clanking cowbells and stopped to shoot several deer grazing on the slopes of the small mountain with the fort topping it in the distance. As they got closer to the southern part of the tiny country, the mountains in Italy seemed to loom over them. Beautiful, rugged, covered with snow and gray rock sparkling in the mid-morning sun. The last farmhouse they had passed was maybe twenty minutes behind them, and it felt as though they were far away from any human or human habitation.

They got to a bend that overlooked the river on the border and stopped to shoot the breathtaking scene of the deep canyon splicing between the mountains. Bri had to tilt her head back to see their peaks. The river was the same one they had seen from the fort, except they were much lower in elevation—the fort was amazingly close, just looming over a narrow chasm between them. Bri could see the tourist-on-a-budget possibilities of the place. Experiencing the beauty of the Alps without experiencing the prices.

Zen pointed to some buildings in a spot low on the mountain that dipped down to the river. "That's where my cousin works. It's the lower part of the resort. The more famous upper part is at the top of that gondola lift, just out of sight from here."

Bri tried to wrap her mind around the idea that she was looking at a magazine-cover picture-perfect scene and Zen saw . . . what did she see? Just another place owned by the family? Someplace normal?

"Have you spent much time there?" Bri asked.

Zen cocked her head. "Because it's the oldest of all our properties, all of us are encouraged to work our first jobs there. I worked there during my sixteenth and seventeenth summers. I wasn't the type to wait tables and greet visitors, or anything public like that. I bussed tables, carried luggage, loaded and unloaded food on the gondolas for the restaurant up top. I admit, I loved the physical activity."

"Did you ever pinch yourself that you worked in such a breathtaking place?"

Zen smiled as she gazed at the valley with what Bri would call fond nostalgia in her eyes. "Every day. I never took the privilege of working there or at any of our properties for granted. I got to know and became friends with people who needed those jobs to survive. The only thing that kept me from feeling too guilty about taking someone's job is that I learned everything I could so we could make their lives better."

"That's pretty thoughtful for a sixteen-year-old."

Zen chuckled. "Blame Great-Grandfather Benbrook for that. He not only wanted all of us to work for a living, he wanted us to devote our lives to helping others in some way or another."

They stashed their main cameras into their packs and climbed back onto the bikes.

"What would he have thought about you doing what many would consider boys' jobs?" Bri asked.

Bri loved Zen's amused smile, as if she delighted in the absurdities of the world. "My aunt Fiona did all those jobs. She turned out okay."

Bri wanted to ask if that was why she'd been fast-tracked into all the high-powered behind-the-scenes running of the company, but it could be a sore spot, since she had quit all that when she was only thirty-four.

They came to another narrower dirt and gravel road that disappeared into dense trees. Zen set her camera right before the road entrance and just for a different angle Bri put hers closer to the outer edge of the road they were on. The setting up and retrieving cameras had become so routine, Bri found herself getting ready to stop at the same time as Zen. She really was learning the tricks of the trade.

"It's not far now," Zen said as they pedaled into the trees, the road dappled with bright spots of light in the shadows from the thick canopy hanging over them.

'Really?" Bri asked. "That wasn't hard to get to."

"Getting electric bikes for tourists was a brilliant idea," Zen said. "It's the easiest, quickest way of getting around, and the country is small enough that you can go anywhere in less than an hour."

Bri glanced at her. "As long as it's not raining."

Zen glanced back. "Remember those little electric trucks?"

"Yes." Bri drew out the word.

"Benbrook has fleets of little electric vans that hold up to six people that would have no problems with these roads. And, of course, they're adaptable to winter use."

"You've thought of everything."

Zen stopped at a small meadow to the side of the road and got off her bike. "We have to walk the bikes the rest of the way."

Bri looked at the clearing and didn't see any rest of the way. She grimaced as they walked the bikes through the grass and weeds, hoping her shoes wouldn't get stained. The meadow opened up and extended to the left where there was a small break in the trees.

Zen leaned her bike against a tree. "It's just up this path."

"Up?" Bri asked, leaning her bike against another tree.

Zen glanced back at her. "Just a short gentle incline."

"Why do I think your idea of a short gentle incline is different from mine?"

Zen laughed. "Let's compare."

She stepped onto the path, and Bri had no choice but to follow. They walked maybe ten feet through the trees and . . . Whoa. Where'd that come from?

Bri was first hit by a thundering din—the thick line of trees must have masked the sound from the road. A steep mountain wall rose from what looked like a chasm in front of them. Water, sparkling and dazzling, cascaded down that wall, crashing hard against plateaus of rugged gray and white rocks.

Bri eased her way to the waist-high rustic stone wall that ran along the cliff edge all the way to the falls. She lifted her camera over the edge to shoot the dizzying scene below. She looked down and forced herself to take in the waterfall creating a rainbow of shimmering mist as the water smashed into a transparent pool that fed into a rocky river that further down the gorge emptied into a larger river that had to be the one on the border. The river bend to Zen's family resort was between them and the fort. She couldn't believe how far down it was.

Bri looked around and blinked at Zen, who was standing about ten feet further up the wall-lined trail. She was manipulating something in her hand. The drone. She was getting a view that none of the others would have when they visited here.

"Now set up your camera in the trees with a direct view to the edge, so you can get a shot of you walking through them and emerging and going to the wall," Zen said.

Right. Need the lead up to the dramatic reveal.

Bri made all the obligatory shots and walked to Zen, who was simply leaning forward with her legs against the wall and gazing at the spectacular scene. She turned and almost stopped Bri's breath with her gentle happy expression and eyes filled with . . . affection? No, that was too strong, but a look no one had ever aimed at her before. Bri blinked out of her silly ideas. Of course, affection. She was looking at a place overflowing with family pride and happy memories.

"So, what do you think?" Zen's eyes danced with amusement.

Bri nodded as if assessing the scene. "Not bad. If you like dramatic plummeting waterfalls."

Zen laughed, and Bri couldn't stop her grin. "There's something even better."

"Better than this?"

"This way." Zen continued down the wall-lined trail, and Bri tried to shoot as she walked. If this was her exclusive, she wanted it to be a vlog that would get consistently high views for years.

The trail and the wall ended to the side of the shower of water. So close, Bri put her fingers in the flow of water. The spray was refreshing.

"The best feature is this way." Zen pointed behind them to what looked like the beginnings of a track surrounded by huge ferns and small trees.

Bri gave it a dubious look.

"It's only about twenty feet," Zen said. "And I bet no one else will find it. Unless we tell them that is."

Hmm. Dangling that exclusive promise in front of her again. Bri had to admit she was curious enough to not need it as an incentive.

Zen stepped back. "I'll stay behind you so you can shoot yourself following the track."

Bri gave her another dubious look, but knew she was being silly. Zen wasn't going to let her do anything dangerous. Bri aimed her camera in front of her and walked to the trail, surprised to see an actual path, obviously kept up. It followed the rocky slope on one side and a flat part on the waterfall side. More intriguing, it curved toward the waterfall. What the . . . ?

A ragged opening in the rock behind the waterfall gaped in front of her. She glanced back at Zen, who was just a few feet behind her.

"Go on," Zen said over the much-louder thundering.

Bri kept her camera steady and stepped through the opening. She was in a sizable cave behind the waterfall. The pocked gray walls danced in blotches of whites and glowing yellows from the sunlight filtering through the cascading. The sound of falling water echoed and, well, thundered as it pounded the water polished stone. She had to find more descriptive words for the vlog. She walked to the middle of the rocky and sandy space and faced a sizable almost rectangular hole where the wall of water plummeted only an arm's length away, every drop catching the sunlight.

She took hesitant steps to the hole that had a natural low barrier between her and the edge of slick stone, mesmerized by the streaming, pounding water and the dancing rainbows caused by the mist puffing into the cave.

Bri turned to Zen, who was shooting different parts of the cave. "I want this to look like a place where people just have to visit."

Zen frowned. "It sells itself."

Bri stared at the falling water and shook her head. "I want to show that I get it."

Zen cocked her head. "My observation about you and nature was only that. An observation. I'm sure no one else has noticed it."

Bri met her eyes. "I have." She just never wanted to admit what she didn't like about her nature footage. The problem wasn't nature. The problem was her. She didn't look natural in nature.

Zen walked up to her and turned to the waterfall. "Then let's see what we can do."

Bri took a few deep breaths. "I just have to embrace the wonder of this place."

Zen gave her a side look. "Are you embracing it now?"

Bri sighed as the fine mist hit her face and gazed at the sunlight sparkling through the stream of water. "In my own way, I guess."

"You have to feel it with more than your head." Zen turned to the opening and lifted her hand into the falls, letting the water pound against it and flow around it. "You have to feel its power and beauty with your touch, with your emotions, with your soul, until it wraps you into a mystical aura."

Bri shook my head. "I was born Bri, not Zen. Practical, not mystical."

Zen faced Bri. "I don't believe you. Think about all the water plummeting and pounding into the rocks below, the power it takes to polish the stone, the wonderful colors created by the clouds of mist . . ."

"I can appreciate all that but . . ." Bri looked up at the dancing mist. "I'm good at doing travelogues for the same reason I was good at being a television reporter. I can be interested without being emotionally invested in the subject."

"But you have to feel an emotional reaction sometime." Zen looked almost despondent.

"I've always been kind of emotionally reserved." Bri shrugged.

"You just haven't tapped deep enough. Allow yourself to feel."

Bri looked up at the misty rainbows. "I'm afraid, this is as deep as I go."

"I don't believe it." Zen wiped her wet hand on her pants.

'It's true." Bri sighed. Maybe not. She could feel her defeat very deeply.

"I refuse to believe it."

Bri tentatively touched the stream of water with her finger. "Well, if you can figure out how to get a shot of me showing a true emotional reaction to this place I'll give you credit for filming it."

"May I have your camera?" Zen asked.

"Sure." Bri handed Zen her camera.

Zen pulled a lightweight tripod from her backpack and put the camera on it. She set the tripod in the sand several feet away from Bri and aimed it at her. She then took what looked like a remote from a pocket on her backpack and pushed buttons back and forth between the remote and the camera.

Zen strode to Bri and before Bri could react, Zen's lips—her soft oh-my-god lips—were gently caressing her's. Bri's logical mind glitched from the sensations on her lips and from Zen's hard muscled body against her. *I can't . . . what was I saying? I . . . I . . .*

Bri, feeling dazed, stared into soft gray eyes.

Zen turned Bri to face the waterfall. She gazed at the sparkles and the rainbows and the endless flow of water. The thunderous pounding almost an echo through her lightheadedness.

"Wow," Bri whispered. Wait. Did she say that out loud?

Bri took in several deep breaths as she pulled herself out of whatever the hell happened and spun around to Zen, who was standing several feet behind her. Zen aimed the remote at the camera and pushed a button.

"What was that?" Bri waved her hands at her. "I can't believe you did that. So . . . So presumptuous."

Zen cocked her head and was to Bri in two steps with her arms around her and her lips assaulting Bri's in the most mind-blowing way. *Oh my god. Stop. Don't stop. St . . .*

Zen pulled away.

Bri gazed into gentle enigmatic eyes. "Okay, maybe not so presumptuous."

With an amused half-grin, Zen went to the camera.

Bri could only stare as Zen removed the camera from the tripod and handed it to her. "Did you get the footage?"

Zen looked up from collapsing the tripod. "Yep."

Bri took a deep breath. She'd sort out her reaction later. "Okay, then."

She went to the cave entrance, glanced back at a grinning Zen, and stepped outside. *Don't say anything, don't babble, just keep your mouth shut . . . she may kiss me again.* She sucked in a breath. *Not that that's a bad thing . . .* She released her breath . . . She was so confused.

Bri

BY THE TIME they got to the gravel road, Bri had forgiven Zen for her unorthodox approach to getting a reaction from her. It didn't stop her from muttering about it all the way to the bicycles, with Zen looking way too amused. But who wouldn't want to be kissed by Zen Benbrook? Bri even gave her major kudos for thinking of the most shocking thing she could do shy of shoving Bri into the falls to get the right reaction on camera.

Shocked. Yeah, that was her reaction . . . but . . . how did Zen figure out her . . . she wasn't going to call it a secret. Just an aspect of herself she had chosen not to disclose as a part of her traveler persona. Actually, she had no problem being herself, so to speak, but she had been encouraged by well-meaning people to keep her private life private and everyone would just assume she was straight. That had been seven years ago, and the world had changed so much since then.

She glanced at Zen, whose attention was on something further up the road. She had been a solo traveler as long as Bri, but she had also been out since she had been a teenager. And nowadays, several gay travelers and even couples had successful vlog channels. Bri knew that they lost followers when they showed their gayness, so to speak, but she also knew they gained followers for the same reason.

She heard voices and frowned. She walked her bike to Zen who had gone a little further up the road, listening.

"That sounds like people yelling in German," Bri said.

"I think some of our colleagues are in trouble." Zen got on her bike and pedaled up the road.

Bri shook her head as she rode after Zen. This country would be great without the people.

They rounded a bend that opened onto a flat expanse of grasses and spring flowers. And men. A lot of men. Maybe thirty of them in rustic farmer-type clothes. Sally, Kristy, and Jon were standing with their bikes in front of the group, engaged in a very spirited conversation.

Zen sighed as she pedaled faster. The others saw her coming and looked beyond relieved. Bri got off her bike and aimed her camera at the scene. Zen had captured her trip to the waterfalls and got the shot Bri had wanted—unconventional method aside. She'd return the favor and capture Zen doing her thing. She wished she had Zen's drones . . . and knew how to use them.

"Oh, thank god," Sally said as Zen got off her bike and walked it to them.

Zen kicked down her kickstand, strode without hesitation to a man in an Alpine cap who seemed to be doing most of the talking, and planted herself in front of him. He glared at her and rattled off something in German with dismissive body language.

Bri joined the others and followed the translation on Kristy's phone. He was basically asking what Zen thought she was doing. He didn't have to listen to her.

"Yes, you do," Zen said in German in her calm steady voice.

Bri exchanged glances with the others as they read the translation on the phone.

"You're a woman. Go find your man. I'll talk to him." The man waved and turned back to Jon.

"Did you vote for Birkhofer?" Zen asked.

The man put up his hand to indicate he wasn't going to talk to her.

"He's not going to talk to you." Zen nodded at Jon. "I'm talking to you. This is what you voted for when you elected Birkhofer to bring Marquardt into the twenty-first century so you can participate in the tourist trade."

The man glared at her. "I did not vote for *this*. We are heading to the government house to protest what is happening in town. Our wives were shocked by what they saw. The ministers promised we'd only get the good tourists, the ones who share our family values."

"Those ministers resigned yesterday."

"They cannot be removed for two more years," a thin man said.

"But they can resign any time they want," Zen said. "And they resigned yesterday."

The man in the cap shook a finger at her. "You're a woman. You don't understand these things."

"She was the chief negotiator for Benbrook for years," Jon said. "She knows more of what she's talking about than almost anyone on this planet."

The men stared at Jon.

"Is this what this"—the man in the cap looked Zen up and down with disdain—"woman, I guess, told you? And you believed her?"

"No, she didn't tell me." Jon folded his arms. "This is information freely available out in the rest of the world."

Bri shook her head. Jon might as well be speaking Greek. The idea of free information was completely foreign to people who had lived for fifty-five years with every single aspect of their lives strictly controlled.

"This is not what we voted for," the man in the cap said. "We're going to complain to the ministers, and you'll be asked to leave."

Zen shrugged. "We're here at your invitation, so you have control over whether we stay or not." She went back to her bike and walked it to the side of the road. Bri and the others quickly lined up next to her to allow the men to pass by.

They stomped by, ignoring the travelers as if they were already gone from their country.

Sally sucked in a breath. "That was pleasant."

Kristy rolled her bike onto the road and faced the others. "You know, I was feeling really optimistic about this place. After talking to those kids last night and seeing all the Benbrook folk this morning, it felt like everything would be okay."

"But now?" Bri asked, feeling a bit deflated herself.

Kristy waved at the retreating men. "How will Birkhofer ever convince them to change?"

"The total population of Marquardt is around seven thousand in about forty-nine square kilometers—like thirty square miles," Zen said. "About five thousand live in and around Marquardt City. Many live above the shops and around courtyards within the city walls. But most live in very ugly apartment blocks near where they're putting in all the fast-food places and new outside businesses. The other two thousand live in the village of Wasserfallschucht and in the farms scattered around the countryside."

Bri frowned. That name sounded a lot like waterfalls.

"Yes, yes." Jon bobbed his head, seeming to return to his natural optimistic buoyancy. "We're just coming back from there. That's where the cheesemaking business is. One of the young men from last night gave us a tour and sold us some cheese." He nodded at a cloth bundle hanging from his handlebars.

"How did the other villagers treat you?" Bri asked.

"They just kind of ignored us," Kristy said. "Not in a rude way. But like acknowledged us and went on doing what they were doing."

"Like Frau Mueller?" Zen asked.

Kristy looked as if she'd been smacked in the face by a clue. "Yes. That's it. Frau Mueller had no problem with us, and you said she wanted to work with your aunt."

"And she's an old-timer." Sally got caught up in the enthusiasm. "What the kids said last night finally makes sense. Their families aren't against us decadent outsiders. They're just reacting like people set in their ways."

"It's the change they're afraid of," Bri said, feeling a kind of relief. "That's why they want the young people to deal with us, rather than forbid them to associate with us evil foreigners."

Zen rolled her bike onto the road. "We got the wrong signals from Viktor because he was trained by the ministers and was following their directives. There is only a small faction of males who don't want to lose their authority over women."

Kristen got on her bike. "I feel so much better now."

"Where are you guys heading?" Sally asked.

"We were going back to town for lunch," Bri said.

"So were we," Jon said as he got on his bike.

"My aunt is making sure her crew eats well and has taken over the hotel restaurant." Zen rode in a circle around them.

"If it's anything like those sandwiches you brought us, I'm in."
Sally ran her bike down the road and threw herself onto it like a
twelve-year-old.

The rest of them followed after her, laughing.

Zen

ZEN TROTTED UP the hotel's stairs. She pushed open the
door to the fifth floor and was confronted by a din of voices and
printers and a hallway with people everywhere, doors propped
open, and the general chaos of trying to do everything at once in a
very short amount of time.

She squeezed around clumps of workers and mobile computer
workstations and passed rooms with people in front of whiteboards
or sheets of paper scattered on beds. She came to a pair of glass
doors that stood open to the gym that served as transition central
and entered the fray. The couple of pieces of gym equipment Fitz
had mustered for the space had been pushed off to the side, and
tables filled with large sheets that looked like blueprints and maps
were laid out on a half-a-dozen worktables.

Zen grinned at Frederica, who was bent over a table talking
steadily and moving her finger over what looked like a mechanical
schematic. She lifted that finger to point at a young man who
nodded, trotted past Zen, and out the door. Frederica's finger
returned to the schematic and pointed to another worker. The night
shift must just be coming to work.

Zen approached the table. "How's life in the trenches?"

Frederica looked up and grinned. "It's the best challenge we've
ever had. So much work to do. So many details. It's glorious."

And she meant it. Frederica loved it when someone told her
something was impossible. She wouldn't sleep until she proved
them wrong.

"I'm glad I was able to make your day." Zen studied the
schematic and saw they were working on all the potential tourist
areas outside of the town, including the fort.

"You made my whole year, maybe even the decade." Frederica
spotted a young woman entering the room and waved her over.

"I'll leave you to it."

Frederica acknowledged her with a wave as she peppered the young woman with questions about the condition of an old farmstead up in the hills.

Zen wandered out into the hall and went to an alcove with some empty chairs and sat in the one next to the window. She pulled out her phone, took a deep breath, and hit Karma's icon.

After a few seconds, Karma appeared on the screen.

"I was expecting your footage," she said.

"You'll get it in a bit," Zen said.

Karma crinkled her nose. "Where are you? Sounds like a crowd."

"Frederica has taken over the fifth floor and is in full battle mode." Zen held the camera so Karma could see the activity in the alcove and hall.

Karma laughed. "She must be in heaven."

"Close to it." Zen took in another breath.

"Spit it out, sis," Karma said.

"I, uh, kissed Bri. Twice."

"What?" Karma glanced around, probably making sure her staff wasn't paying attention. "How'd that happen?"

"Well, that has something to do with some of the footage I'll be sending," Zen said. "I want the trip to the waterfall footage not to be used in today's vlog."

"Okay." Karma drew out the word.

"I offered Bri an exclusive to vlog about the waterfall first," Zen said. "The other travelers only found out about it tonight."

Karma laughed. "You bribed her for a kiss?"

"No." Zen pulled her head back, surprised. "I'm not that clever. She kind of set herself up for it." She explained the whole adventure in kissing to a very amused Karma.

"So, she didn't slap you into next week," Karma said.

"She didn't." Zen was still working out Bri's reaction. "I'm trying to control my optimism but I'm afraid she took the kisses at face value . . . Me taking on her dare to get an emotional response out of her and answering her challenge that I was being presumptuous. But I think she knows that I know she's gay."

"Okay." Karma looked thoughtful. "Well, I don't have to warn you about treading carefully."

Zen looked out at the chaos around her. "You know, now that I'm getting to know her, I'm, I don't know, I'm not as anxious about all my feelings and stuff." She looked at Karma. "I'm actually enjoying just palling around with her."

Karma grinned. "You're mellowing in your old age."

Zen laughed. "Maybe I finally found someone who I like, instead of just lusting after."

"Well, you were bound to finally become a mature human being some time," Karma said.

Zen smirked. "Thanks, sis. But I left the mature part behind when I decided to walk for a living."

"Ah, but we can't stop getting older." Karma glanced at something to her side. "Oops. Work is calling."

"I'll get the footage to you in a while." Zen held up a finger. "And check out Bri's channel. Let me know what you think about her team."

Karma smirked. "I don't even want to know what's going through your mind."

Zen shrugged. "Just working on some contingency plans."

"Uh-huh." Karma shook her head. "But I'll check out her channel." She glanced around. "Gotta go. Later." She waved and the screen went black.

Zen stared at that blackness for several moments as she processed the idea that she really wasn't the same person who had dated all the trendy women because they were beautiful and fun. She had never considered having any kind of life with them. They had been passing fancies. Bri was nothing like them. Not even remotely.

She blinked up and gazed at the people buzzing around, spending long hours performing miracles for the company. Maybe she *was* finally becoming a mature human being.

Bri

BRI SAT DOWN at the computer, not knowing where to start. It had been the fullest day yet. She pulled the memory cards from the cameras and copied the files to the computer. Zen had the key footage of the day. She glanced at Zen, who was efficiently copying and uploading her files.

They had a fun rest of the day. To begin with, the food in the restaurant was so much better now. Fresh and simple salads, soups, and sandwiches.

The eight of them had joined forces and biked around town to see the progress of the Benbrook crew. More locals were also out, watching their town transform before their eyes. Their skepticism seemed to change to curiosity to just short of excitement. It turned out, they had been more afraid of the ministers because they had spent their lives being afraid of them.

They then did a bike tour of the mundane part of town. The drab apartment blocks were as frigid as any cold war architecture, the street of fast-food joints and modern construction was on its way to looking like any off-the-highway main street in America.

Never in a million years would Bri have thought she'd be so comfortable around these people she viewed as competitors for followers. They were just people who happened to be travel vloggers. They didn't even seem to have her obsession with getting and keeping followers.

She glanced at Zen again. The last couple of days, Bri had caught Zen casually looking at her and winking at odd times. Today, Bri found herself watching her, as much as she tried not to. She frowned and turned her chair to face Zen.

Zen looked her way. "Do you need the files now?"

Bri could only stare at her, unable to articulate what she wanted to say. She didn't even know what she wanted to say.

Zen's eyes widened with concern, and she rolled her chair to Bri. She turned Bri's chair around so they faced each other. "What's wrong? Is it the kisses? I'm sorry if they—"

Bri gave her head a shake. "It's not that . . . Well, it is that . . . But . . ." She took a deep breath. What was she trying to say? "You kiss me twice and act like it's nothing. The first one was because I all but dared you, and that was a brilliant solution to what I wanted. The second was because I challenged you . . ." She flopped her hands around, as if that was going to focus her confused brain. "I guess . . . I don't know . . . It's back to ordinary me . . ."

Zen grabbed Bri's hand. She looked so alarmed, Bri snapped out of whatever was floundering around in her brain.

"You're anything but ordinary," Zen said. "If I could I'd kiss you every minute of the day."

Bri was pretty sure her jaw was hanging open as she stared, stunned, at her.

Zen looked a bit sheepish. "I, uh, was hoping you had been invited on this venture."

"What?"

Zen gazed at the floor. "I'm not sorry I kissed you, but I had promised myself I wouldn't do anything"—she shrugged—"stupid around you."

"What?" Bri's brain was in a chaotic swirl.

Zen sighed as she looked up at Bri. "I, uh, I have a massive crush on you . . . From watching your vlogs."

"What?" Bri couldn't have been more shocked than if Zen had slapped her. She was not crush material by any measure. Much less massive. Massive?

"I started watching your vlogs and found myself looking forward to the next one. I just . . ." She captured Bri's eyes, kind of shy and embarrassed. "I just hoped our paths would cross one day."

Bri put her hands over her face as she processed a turn of events stranger than anything she'd ever encountered in her travels. Zen Benbrook, who had, at least in her younger days, several very famous, very glamorous, very beautiful girlfriends, had a massive crush on her? Ordinary, not even bordering on cute or interesting looking, her?

Zen gazed at Bri, concern in her eyes. She gently pulled Bri's hands from her face and wrapped her hands around them. "I understand if you don't feel the same. I just wanted you to know that those kisses weren't just to get a reaction. I'd been wanting to kiss you since the moment I saw you in the village."

Bri willed herself not to say "What?" again. Wanting to kiss her? Really wanting to kiss her? Wait. Feel the same? Why would she feel the same . . . ? Oh god. She sucked in much needed air. It wasn't as if she couldn't keep her eyes off of Zen. It wasn't as if she'd absorbed as much as she could about her and religiously watched every one of her vlogs, even as she told herself it was for research and to know what her rival was doing so she could strategize around it. It wasn't that she couldn't get enough of her gentle voice and the way her simple hiking clothes clung to her muscular body . . . *Oh my god.*

"Uh." Bri finally articulated something other than "what." "It's not that I . . . I mean . . . It's not that I don't like you . . . I mean . . . ."

Zen leaned forward and gently kissed her.

Bri blinked at her. "I don't find your kisses unpleasant or anything . . . ."

Zen had a kind of half smile that was mostly in her eyes reflecting a gentle amusement mixed with affection that Bri loved seeing in her vlogs. It was the kind of look Bri always wished someone would give her someday . . . And now there it was. Only for her.

Tears pooled in Bri's eyes. *What the . . . ?* She pulled her hands from Zen's and turned away. She didn't cry for anything. She inherited some kind of stoic gene that she couldn't even cry when it was completely appropriate.

"Would you be willing to start this new journey with me?" Zen asked. "The first step, just getting to know each other?"

Bri wiped away the tears and turned back to Zen, whose expression was now gentle and solemn and full of affection. How could anyone on the planet resist that look? Or maybe that was just Bri. Maybe she couldn't resist because she *was* attracted to her.

"I've been told I'm not the easiest traveling companion or the easiest person to get along with for that matter," Bri said.

The amusement returned to Zen's eyes. She retook Bri's hands. "A part of the journey is learning how to match our steps."

Bri gazed at her in wonder. Could it be as simple as that? They lived completely different lifestyles. On completely different planets. She couldn't envision how just starting this journey could work after they left Marquardt.

"If we want it to work, we'll make it work," Zen said. "Even if we end up just good friends, I think my life will be much richer with you in it."

Oh my god. How had any woman resisted her gentle onslaught of charm?

"Are you going to keep kissing me?"

Zen slyly smiled. "Do you want me to?"

No. Yes. She couldn't believe she was even having this conversation with herself or with Zen. She took a deep breath. "Yes."

Was this what they meant by getting swept off one's feet? Because Bri felt as if her feet had been swept under her and if she wasn't in a chair, she'd be sitting on the floor.

9
Day Five

Zen

ZEN WANDERED AROUND the room, waiting for Frederica to get back to her. She had seen them unload two electric mini-vans and had promised the group they would test them on the back roads. But Frederica had to okay it, and her current priorities were much more important.

Bri emerged from the bathroom, brushing her hair, and frowned at Zen. "Do you ever stop walking?"

Zen shrugged. "I always seem to have too much energy and have to move to burn it off."

"Sounds exhausting." Bri went to her desk and pulled her batteries from their chargers, loaded them into her cameras, and put the spares in her bag.

Zen tried not to grin at how quickly Bri had picked up the mundane routines of a solo vlogger. Her phone buzzed, and she put it to her ear. "Hi."

"Good idea about testing the mini-vans," Frederica said. "Greg's bringing them up to the front for you."

"Thank you, Auntie." Zen gave Bri a thumbs up. "I'll let you know how they work."

"Sounds good. Gotta go."

Zen ended the call. "We got the vans."

"Excellent." Bri shouldered her pack. "Breakfast first."

Zen laughed as she shouldered her own backpack. "If we get lucky, we'll be able to eat in Wasserfallschucht for lunch."

Bri opened the door and looked back at her. "About that name. Sounds a lot like waterfalls."

Zen nodded as she followed Bri into the hall. "It's named after its close-by landmark."

"Which everyone else will be visiting today," Bri said. "That was a great story about us learning about the falls from a local while we were biking around."

"Kind of true," Zen said. "I used to be the local who saw the falls from the river road across the border."

Bri frowned. "How'd you know about the cave?"

"The old-timers used to talk about hiking around Marquardt before the borders were closed and going to the falls and visiting the cave."

"Hmm." Bri looked as if she was musing about something as they walked down the hallway. "I'm not sure whether to thank them or not."

Zen grinned. She certainly thanked them . . . a million times over.

Bri

"I THINK YOU missed a pothole." Mick looked back at the road from the front passenger seat of the tiny six-person van with the top folded down.

"I didn't see you volunteering to drive," Sally said as she deftly avoided a long rut in the gravel and dirt road.

"We need to add road improvement to the list," Bri said.

Zen looked up from replacing the battery in her drone. "I'm sure Frederica has already put together a master plan for it."

"Your family is better than a well-regulated militia," Sally said.

Zen grinned. "We're lucky Fiona and Frederica inherited their grandfather's drive for perfection and organizational genius."

"Amen to that." Sally jerked on the small steering wheel. "Hang on."

Bri and Zen grabbed the bars attached to the back of the front seats as they swayed with the bumps.

The van ahead of them almost swerved off the road, revealing a small trench down the middle.

"What are they driving on these roads?" Mick half-stood to study the trench as Sally maneuvered around it.

"They're coming off of winter," Zen said. "Sledges do a number on unpaved roads. I'm surprised they haven't repaired the worst of them by this time. Especially this road."

"Another guided trip to one of their treasured landmarks on a barely passable road by someone who never took driving lessons?" Sally shook her head.

The van ahead stopped next to a clearing.

Jon, behind the wheel, stood and turned around. "Is this the place?"

"Yes," Zen said.

Kristy jumped out of the other van and looked around. "Add parking lot to your list," she said to Bri.

Bri gave a thumbs up. She kind of liked being the list person and having a special place within the group. A group she never thought she'd want to be a part of, much less have fun in their company.

Maybe she'd been wrong treating her fellow travelers as competition rather than peers. She never shook her competitive attitude from when she worked for the television station in central Illinois. Where she had done local features, very popular with the viewers, but not with the budget-cutting powers that be. She and her team, Sarah and Josh, had been a part of a slash-and-burn downsizing. Popularity wasn't stronger than the bottom line.

The irony was, her total income from her travel vlog and all the offshoots from it—merchandise, sponsors, affiliate marketing—was more than the three of them had made from working for that television station combined, which allowed them to actually make a full-time living from vlogging.

Sally pulled up behind the other van and everyone gathered on the grassy area off the road.

Bri looked at the trees in the direction of the waterfall, listening for pounding water. Maybe a whisper but she really couldn't hear it. She pulled out her notebook and added to her list to put this acoustical phenomenon on the future informational display at the trailhead to the waterfall.

"The trail starts between those two trees." Zen pointed to the other side of the clearing. "The path to the cave is off of where the main trail ends."

Bri and Zen watched the others disappear up the trail. As they stood there, Bri was very aware of Zen's presence next to her and was, once again, at her mercy for whatever they were doing that day.

Zen turned to her. "Ready to visit Wasserfallschucht?"

On the other hand, it'd been fun seeing the sights with Zen, and she knew how to find the special details. Bri gave her a speculative look. "Any more exclusives up your sleeve?"

Zen shrugged. "I guess that's something we'll discover together."

"So, no special research?" Bri asked as they sauntered back to their mini-van.

"A tiny village that looks more Italian than Marquardtian, winding narrow lanes up and down the side of the mountain." Zen climbed into the driver side as Bri settled on the passenger seat. "It's on the side of the mountain that towers over the tributary the waterfalls spills into."

"But you can't see the waterfall from there." Bri grabbed the frame above her as Zen pulled onto the road and continued past the clearing.

Zen flashed her a quizzical look.

"The others would have seen it."

Zen nodded. "Maybe they just didn't know where to look."

Bri turned to her. "Ah hah. You do have some inside info."

Zen laughed. "My aunt's troops have been scouting before conquering. But I've heard there's a place from which you can see the waterfall. I just don't know where it is."

"I guess we'll have to explore the whole town then." Bri looked ahead, knowing Zen was flashing her more quizzical looks. Once she got used to the idea that Zen really had a crush on her—as absurd as it sounded—she found herself wanting to have some fun with it. Which was so out of character for her. Maybe it was the thin mountain air.

They rambled past the place where they had confronted the angry men—hard to believe it had been only the day before. Now the only sounds above the whispering whine of the electric

engine were birds and the swishing of the spring grasses. And—
Bri shaded her eyes as she studied movement on a rise of land—
goats with bells around their necks, adding a sparkle among the
wildflowers. She remembered to keep the camera going for lots
of B-roll footage. It may never be used but could never be re-
captured. Something Zen had said. Unlike film in the old days,
memory space was free.

A new noise penetrated the pastorale sounds. Zen half-stood,
keeping her hands on the wheel, as she gazed at something down
the road.

She sat down with a grin. "The invading forces are headed this
way."

Sunlight flashed off of something, and a mini-truck rolled into
view flanked by burgundy and white t-shirted workers on electric
bikes. As they neared, Bri counted three more mini-trucks and a
dozen more bicycles followed by maybe twenty, mostly young
people, on foot.

Zen pulled over onto the entrance to a path.

"Have a fun makeover?" Zen asked as the convoy stopped next
to the mini-van.

"Yep." The driver of the lead truck looked around at her
beaming crew. "One of the more scenic places we've worked in.
Plus, the people are friendlier than in the city." She leaned toward
Zen and Bri. "I got an inkling they've had a lot of unauthorized
interaction with their Italian neighbors over the years."

Zen chuckled. "I'm sure they know all the ways to slip in and
out of Italy through the gorge."

"Made our job easier," the driver said. "Enjoy your visit and let
us know if we need to do anything else."

"Will do," Zen said as the envoy's engines whined to life and
the buoyant, laughing group rode and marched past them.

"Is a positive attitude a prerequisite for a job in your company?"
Bri asked as Zen eased the van back onto the road.

Zen glanced at her. "In a way, I guess it is."

"Meaning?" Bri grabbed the frame above her as they navigated
an especially treacherous patch of road.

Zen waggled her head. "Most people don't last long in the
company without a positive attitude. They have to really enjoy
all aspects of the hospitality business. Most of the employees

doing this transition are from our creative, engineering, and maintenance departments, plus a bunch of youngsters who are either seasonal and this is a way of picking up extra money off-season or volunteers from our various properties."

"Must be a good company to work for," Bri said, half to herself.

"Old man Benbrook truly believed in the idea of happy employee, happy company, and it's written into our bylaws to treat every employee as if they were a family member. This means good pay, good benefits, and never taking them for granted."

They came to a split in the road. One branch looked as if it was angling downward and the other upward around a bend.

"Up or down?" Bri asked.

"Believe it or not, down." Zen steered the mini-van to the left and after a small switchback through a grove of trees, the scene opened onto a spectacular rolling meadow with the snowy mountains rising up behind it.

Zen stopped as they stared at the scene. Breathtaking. Too cliché. Bri wanted her description to sound the way she felt looking at it. Her words, her feelings . . .

The wildflowers—purples, whites, yellows—bobbing in the breeze through waving long grasses of every shade of green. An impossibly blue sky setting off the sparkling rugged mountain peaks . . .

Bri blinked as something inside needed to burst out. She couldn't even take a breath.

"Are you okay?"

Bri turned to Zen. "I don't know."

Zen hopped out of the van and trotted around to the passenger side. She slipped her hand under Bri's elbow and helped her out. "Let's walk a little."

Zen offered her arm, and Bri stared at it a moment then locked her arm around it.

They strolled down the road as Bri breathed in the competing scents of the flowers and the grasses. The gentle sounds of swishing grass, chattering birds, the whisper of their shoes on the hard-packed dirt . . .

Bri shook her head. "You probably think I'm some kind of nut case."

Zen chuckled. "I think you haven't given yourself the time to just, well"—she spread out her free arm—"smell the flowers."

Bri took a deep breath. "It just hit me. I not only saw this scene. I felt it. Here." She patted her chest. "I want to find my own words to describe not only what I'm seeing, but what I'm feeling."

Zen looked around and grabbed Bri's hand. "Let's walk through the meadow." She took a step.

Bri didn't budge as she stared at the edge of the almost knee-high grass. "What? There's no path."

Zen playfully tugged her hand. "It's just grass and wildflowers. Soft and beautiful."

"They'll stain my jeans." Bri looked down at herself.

"The hotel has washing machines." Zen wrapped both her hands around Bri's and gave her an irresistible "pretty please" in her eyes. "Just take one step."

Bri allowed herself to be tugged to the edge of the grass. Zen released Bri's hands and walked into long blades of grass, creating a little path. Bri stepped into the cleared area and shifted so her jeans didn't touch the grass.

"It's not going to bite you." Zen held out her hand to Bri.

"That's not what I'm afraid of," Bri muttered but took Zen's hand. She wasn't going to admit she was drawn to the magic of the rolling hills of sparkling wildflowers.

Holding Bri's hand behind her back and pulling her along, Zen forged a narrow path deeper into the meadow. Bri concentrated on where her feet were stepping and ran into Zen, who had stopped walking.

Zen released Bri's hand and turned to steady her with a hand on each arm. Bri gazed at her, caught in her gentle eyes.

"Look around," Zen said.

Bri tore her eyes away from Zen's and took in the sea of grass and wildflowers flowing out around them. They were on top of a small hill, and it felt as if they were in some enchanted scene with the greens and the impossibly blue sky against the towering gray stone mountains streaked with snow. She could see it. Really see it. Everything sparkled like polished diamonds in the clean mountain air.

She turned to Zen, who was a few steps away aiming a camera at her.

Zen lowered the camera. "I think your followers are going to love this new nature-loving Bri."

Bri gazed at the scene around her. "Why didn't I see all this before?"

Zen sent one of her drones up into the air. "You saw it before, but you didn't feel it."

"But why have I never felt it?" Bri ran her hand over a bunch of tall white flowers.

Zen answered with an enigmatic smile.

Zen

ZEN PARKED THE mini-van in a clearing next to the road just outside the gate of the walled village of Wasserfallschucht. A watch tower rose up above the gate, tall enough to most likely allow a view of the river gorge between the countries. The rounded opening in the wall was barely a single lane wide. Zen made a note to recommend putting the parking lot further down the wall, so the entrance to the village wasn't blocked by vehicles. The gate with the tower was one of the more unique and picturesque manmade things she'd seen so far in Marquardt.

The sounds of nature and the stillness of the moss-encrusted stone gave the impression of an abandoned ancient site that was reinforced by what looked like a tunnel through the gate, slightly angled so they couldn't see what was on the other side. Of course, just hours before, the village had been bustling with Benbrook workers, probably lit up like daytime all night.

Bri looked around while getting her backpack from the rear of the van. "It's so peaceful. Are you sure this is the place?"

I've seen Wassesrfallschucht from Italy," Zen said. "It cascades down the cliff almost to the tributary at the bottom of the waterfall."

Bri frowned. "Cascades."

Zen hefted her pack onto her back. "I'm sure there are many horizontal lanes." She walked around the van to Bri. "Knowing my family, they've installed benches everywhere. We can explore at our own pace and as much as we want."

Bri nodded. "Okay. People live here. How bad can it be?"

Zen bit her lip. She didn't want to deter Bri from visiting the town.

"I'll let you walk in first, so I won't be in your frame," Zen said.

Bri gave her a sidelong look.

Zen shrugged. "You'll be the first to see the town after the Benbrook invasion."

Bri held her look a few seconds longer but couldn't stop the bit of amusement in her eyes. She turned to the gate. "Let's see what a Benbrook makeover looks like."

They approached the rounded archway, and Zen stayed a few steps behind as Bri walked into a tunnel of stone and stopped as she looked up at the light stone arched above them. "I feel like I'm going back several hundred years."

"This part of the country feels very rich in history," Zen said.

Bri continued through the tunnel and was flanked by a pair of low buildings that looked like guard huts before walking onto a rectangular courtyard with a quaint curio shop in front of her and small information kiosks where lanes rambled off on either side.

The door of the shop opened and a young man, followed by an older man, both wearing Wassesrfallschucht T-shirts, emerged with welcoming grins.

"Willkommen," they said as they hurried across the courtyard to them.

"We have guides and maps for you," the young man said in English.

"Thank you," Bri said, looking bemused as she and Zen followed them into the shop.

Zen took in the large space with ample room to accommodate milling tourists around the tables that would soon be filled with Marquardt and Wasserfallschucht merchandise by the time the border was open.

"What was this place before?" Zen asked in German.

"It was used for meetings or weddings or whenever someone needed a space like this," the older man said. "The central part of town is further down."

"Is this your place?" Zen asked.

"Yes," the man said. "My family has owned this property for generations."

"Lucky you," Zen said. "Tourists are going to love Wasserfallschucht."

The man exchanged optimistic looks with the younger man. "We hope so."

"I know I'll be back for a T-shirt." Zen nodded at the man's shirt.

"Me too," Bri said.

Zen turned to see Bri had been following the conversation with her phone translator.

"For now, we'll have the pamphlet and the map." Zen had seen the pamphlets and maps compiled and printed on the fifth floor the night before.

"Which way?" Bri asked as they stood in the courtyard.

Zen studied the map and turned to the lane that didn't disappear down the cliff. "This way."

While Marquardt City had a rather stodgy feel to it, Wasserfallschucht was like the fancy-free cousin with stone buildings painted in bright pastels and colorful doors and window shutters that clung to either side of the narrow lanes with offshoots of steep stairs and narrower pathways. Plateaus scalloped from the cliff face revealed hidden courtyards and lanes widening enough to allow for a few tables and chairs outside the small cafes and restaurants that hinted at more than locals visiting the village.

Zen wouldn't be surprised if there wasn't at least one hidden tunnel up from the river that the locals on the other side of the river had used for centuries. Why should a closed border and rigid regime get in the way of a visit to the scenic cliff village?

"It's so different from the town," Bri said after they had wandered in and out of shops, watched a cheesemaking demonstration, and visited the several viewpoints of the river valley and mountains. "And the people are as close to normal as any we've met in this place."

"There are benefits of being a remote place, even in a country as small as Marquardt." Zen stopped at a small sign.

"What's it say?" Bri asked.

"It says, secret garden." Zen peered down a narrow set of steps squeezed between moss-covered rough stone buildings.

"Sounds intriguing," Bri said.

Zen put out her hand. "After you."

Bri pressed record on the GoPro attached to the ribbon on her fedora and carefully walked down the worn steps. The mossy, ancient walls rose up as they rounded a bend, and the steps seemed to plunge them into another world. Bri aimed her main camera up at the towering wall as she walked.

Zen loved the ancient aura that touched all her senses, even the mossy odor, rich, organic, alive. She hoped Bri was feeling it. Feeling the magic. She smiled. Yes, this was a moment of spontaneous magic. The air practically sparkled with it.

Bri stopped at the bottom of the steps at a door made of twisted iron. A wooden plank hung at an angle from a chain with German words in fancy script on it.

She turned to Zen. "What's it say?"

Zen grinned. "It says, 'enter and be enchanted.'"

"Hmmm." Bri pulled the metal bolt. "I'll reserve judgment on that until after I experience it."

Zen put her arm out, leaning close to Bri in the tight area, and pushed the door open. Bri gave her a look, but her eyes couldn't hide her amusement as she walked into the garden.

Zen followed her in delight. She was enjoying this more relaxed, flirty side of Bri.

She looked around in wonder at a smallish courtyard that was a study in dainty strands of green punctuated with tiny pastel flowers draped over delicate whimsical sculptures of metal, stone, and ceramic.

"It's like a fairyland." Bri aimed her camera around the courtyard.

"Hmmm. Almost magical." Zen put her drone on a low wall, and it lifted to about ten feet.

Bri gave her a sidelong look. "Too obvious for spontaneous magic."

Zen shrugged. "Magic is magic. We have to take it when we get it."

Bri frowned as she walked to what looked like an opening on the far side of the courtyard. "Well, I'm holding out for the spontaneous variety." A sign, like the one on the gate was attached to the wall next to the opening. "What does it say?"

Zen took in the words on the sign. "Interesting."

"What?" Bri peered into the opening.

"There's a stained-glass sculpture that captures filtered light," Zen said. "That light is there to illuminate couples who want to have a few minutes of privacy."

Bri flashed her a skeptical look. "Really?"

"Not a surprise, I promise." Zen unfolded the map. "The sign is translated here."

Bri took the map and saw that all the signs had been translated into English on the map. "Well, the stained glass sounds interesting."

Bri stepped into the opening and disappeared around a sharp corner. Zen brought down her drone and paused in the rounded entryway to a narrow stone tunnel. The stone walls were polished and clean, in contrast to the earthy chaos of the garden. She rounded the corner to face an immediate zag that zigged into a small circular space with walls filled with mosaics of painted tiles and shards of colored glass.

Bri stood on a circle of dark stone surrounded by lighter stone in the middle of the chamber. She was bathed in dancing colors and washes of sunlight as she stared up into a shaft that opened to the sky. Zen let her camera linger as Bri seemed to transcend into a sparkling ethereal being. Breathtaking. Magical. Sheer magic.

Bri turned, and her eyes widened as she stared at Zen. Zen realized she was also bathed in the sparkling-colored light.

"Uh, cool." Bri dropped her eyes as if embarrassed for staring.

Zen sucked in a deep breath, took a step closer to the middle of the circle, and looked up. "Wow." She pointed her camera at the array of colored glass and tiles that sifted rays of light around a narrow shaft that opened to the sky.

"I would have never imagined something like this in a place with strict ideas about women. They probably had bars over the entrance so young couples couldn't enter." Bri ran her hand over the tiles, painted with bright alpine scenes.

"I think the residents are rather proud of this slightly scandalous piece of history, and it was probably one of the many things that kept the more conservative citizens from coming here and catching all the nefarious border activity." Zen wandered to the opposite wall and studied the tiles. "This dates back to the fourteenth century, according to the guide, with the stained glass and tiles added in the eighteenth century."

Bri turned and squinted at her. "When did you read the guide?"

Zen shrugged but was delighted by Bri's powers of observation. "I saw it last night when they were being printed."

Bri put her hands on her hips. "So, you did know about this place."

"I only glanced through the guide. I didn't note where things were. I didn't know this was in a secret garden. I thought it was off one of the lanes." Zen shrugged. "Karma's the detail person in the family. I like to be more spontaneous."

"That I *do* believe." Bri clipped her second GoPro onto the strap of her backpack. "I wonder how many times young couples have been caught in here by another couple."

"I guess that was a part of the adventure and danger of sneaking into here," Zen said.

"Hmmm." Bri looked up at the stained glass again.

Zen hid her grin as she walked to the narrow tunnel. "So . . . I guess we should get out of here."

Bri emitted a strangled noise.

Zen stopped, pleasantly surprised and completely delighted that Bri took the bait. She turned with an innocent look, trying not to laugh at Bri's exasperated expression. "I thought you didn't like surprises."

"You . . . you . . ." Bri muttered, her frustration almost comical.

Zen strode to Bri and put her hands on the wall on either side of Bri's head, leaned in, and captured her lips. She couldn't believe how soft and sweet those lips were. Her breath caught as Bri wrapped her arms around her and kissed her back. The small space and the shafts of light created a blanket around them as Zen got lost in the sweetest sensations she'd ever experienced.

Zen found herself gazing into eyes that looked as dazed and amazed as she knew hers were. The air seemed to vibrate with whatever was flowing between them. Zen pulled Bri's hand to her lips and kissed it, then interlaced their fingers. She led Bri through the narrow tunnel back into the garden.

The rest of their group was probably wandering the town looking for them, which didn't give them much time for one more surprise . . . Zen tugged Bri to a small sign on a post in the overgrown far corner of the garden.

"Just an arrow," Bri said.

"Which means they don't have to say what it's pointing to," Zen said.

Bri peeked at a narrow path with a brambly arbor arching over it. "You think this is it?"

Zen shrugged. "It makes sense."

Bri aimed her camera down the path and took a step into the tunnel. "This is really kind of cool."

Zen followed her and focused her camera on the buds of the spindly vines and breathed in the woody scent. Spring was well on its way. The sun broke through the branches as the path spread into a sizable balcony with a waist-high stone wall along the outer edge.

Bri eagerly went to the wall and looked out to the left. Her delighted grin told Zen they had been right. She sat half-turned on the low wall next to Bri and gazed at the tower of cascading water further down the valley and then lifted her gaze to Bri.

"Would any of this qualify as spontaneous magic?" Zen asked.

Bri turned and blinked down at her. She opened her mouth and then frowned. "Maybe some parts."

Zen couldn't help her Cheshire Cat smile. "Some parts?"

Bri cocked her head. "Some parts more than others."

"It *is* a secret garden," Kirsty exclaimed from behind them.

Zen and Bri exchanged it-was-nice-while-it-lasted looks. They continued to gaze at the waterfall, enjoying a few more minutes of the lingering magic before reality intruded.

Bri

BRI PULLED HER videos off the memory cards and glanced at Zen, who was doing the same. She put together her spreadsheet and glanced at Zen, who was working in her efficient focused way. She typed in all the info into the spreadsheet, trying not to glance at Zen.

She let out a sigh and turned her chair to face Zen.

Zen completed a task, took one look at Bri, spun her chair around, and pushed it to her. "What's wrong?"

"I . . . I . . ." Bri sucked in a deep breath. "What's next?"

Zen frowned. "Next as in now?"

Bri waved her hand. "Now, tonight, tomorrow, after tomorrow . . . I don't do spontaneous very well . . . I need . . . I need to know where this is going?"

Zen gazed at Bri as she took her hand. "What are your plans after this?"

"We all decided to take a small break from travel vlogging. Susan and Josh are back home in Illinois where they've been doing my videos, and then we'll all have three more weeks before we set off again." Bri looked down at their hands. "I was going to go back home and relax."

"Okay." Zen nodded. "I can present a few options. But before I do . . . This is going to sound weird, especially from me . . . but I want our first time—if we have a first time—to be as special as you are."

"What?"

"I don't want this to be just another travel romance," Zen said. "I want this to be the beginning of a true romance. If you don't want a relationship, then I hope we can be great friends."

Bri flopped back into the seat. As hard as it had been for her to believe, Zen seemed to really mean what she said about a journey together. And much to her own surprise, she was hoping Zen knew a way to make it happen. "Okay. So, what are the options?"

Zen smiled and lifted Bri's hand to her lips. "Well, if you want to just be really good friends, you can get on your train, and I'll walk back down the hill."

Bri raised an eyebrow.

"Or"—Zen softly caressed the back of Bri's hand with her thumb—"I can get on the train with you wherever you're going and find a nice romantic place to hang out in for a while."

Bri sat up. "You'd get on a train?"

Zen gazed at her. "Yes. For you, anything."

Bri slumped down.

"Or, I could order a car to come from the villa in the valley to pick us up," Zen said.

Bri squinted at her. "You'd take a car?"

"Yes. As I said. For you, anything?"

"Any other options?"

Zen leaned forward and gave Bri a gentle kiss. "We can walk to the villa."

The reality washed over Bri that she had to make a really important decision. She could have told Zen at any time she wasn't interested in anything other than friendship . . . but she hadn't. Because she was interested in Zen. She just wasn't ready for such a sudden change . . . but this kind of thing was always a sudden change.

"So, we either part ways as friends or end up at my place or yours so to speak . . . and then what?" Bri asked.

"Well, I might accompany you back to the States, to visit my sister . . . She might want to meet your team. She was very impressed with the production of your vlogs."

"Really?" Bri had to admit she was worried about how she and Zen could keep up their travel schedules and find time together, but if she didn't have to worry about Susan and Josh not having work . . . Josh had been impressed by Zen's vlogs and always liked her channel. He was also practically giddy from all the great footage from Zen.

"Yeah." Zen cocked her head. "Maybe we can do some collaborative things. Stuff like that."

"Yeah. Maybe." Bri squeezed Zen's hand. "I have a lot to think about." She looked up. "It's not you. It's me. I have problems with change, spontaneity, making important decisions . . ."

Zen stood, bringing Bri up with her, wrapped her arms around her, and pressed her lips to Bri's ear. "It's taking every ounce of my willpower not to sweep you to that bed over there and make mad love to you all night. Just so you know how special you are to me."

Oh my god. Bri sucked in a breath as she clung to Zen's warm strong body. "Are you trying to kill me?"

Zen laughed, kissed Bri's cheek, and stepped away.

10
Day 6
Bri

BRI AND ZEN joined Mick and Joe in the almost empty lobby on the way to the restaurant. The quiet was too much like the first morning they went to breakfast. Where were all the Benbrook people?

"Can you believe it's our last full day here?" Mick asked. "I feel like we need another week to get to know the new tourist-ready Marquardt."

Joe nodded. "I may take Birkhofer up on his invitation to come back for another free visit."

"Wait about three months," Zen said. "I think the atmosphere and the experience will be very different by then."

"It's already different, thanks to your family." Mick stopped at the restaurant entrance. "Whoa."

Bri looked around him at the sea of burgundy and white at every table and crowding the sides.

"This is the whole crew," Zen said. "All hands for the final push."

They carefully made their way around the tables and servers with trays of food to their table, where the other four were already seated.

"I didn't get the memo that it was burgundy and white day," Sally said as Bri settled next to her.

"At least you don't clash with it." Bri looked down at her yellow shirt.

"Looks like Zen got waylaid." Jon lifted his chin in Zen's direction.

A pair of young women were gesturing and talking in excited Italian to Zen, who wore her polite, passive expression. Zen nodded and said something to which the young women responded with delight and numerous *grazies* as they backed away to let Zen continue to the table.

Bri looked up from pouring coffee as Zen settled next to her. "What was that about?"

"A couple of seasonal workers who work at Benbrook Resort." Zen put a tea bag in a pot of steaming water. "They were telling how a bunch of them held a walking race from the lower resort to the upper resort then back down to the lower resort a few weeks ago. They petitioned to make it an annual event for Benbrook staff."

"And they want to name it after you?" Bri exchanged an amused look with Sally.

"Of course, they do," Mick said.

Zen sighed. "I guess I can't stop them because my aunt thinks it's a great idea."

Bri grinned as the others laughed.

The din around them quieted, and Bri looked toward the door and did a double take. A taller, older version of Zen in white jeans and a Burgundy T-shirt stood in the doorway, next to an equally tall woman who could be her sister . . . in fact . . . Bri turned to Zen, who was staring at the women.

"Relatives, I presume," Joe said.

Zen emitted a laugh. "Aunt Fiona is the one in the blue jeans. Aunt Frederica is the general of this army."

"Did you know Fiona was coming here?" Bri asked.

Zen shook her head. "I'm not surprised though. She could hardly keep herself away."

Frederica lifted what looked like a small megaphone to her mouth. "Greetings, everyone."

Bri turned to Zen. "I wasn't expecting a British accent."

Zen chuckled. "Karma and I are the outliers."

"Fiona and I did an early morning stroll around the town"—Frederica half turned to Fiona—"and, I have to say, you've outdone yourselves in transforming this country into a place tourists will be happy to visit."

A grinning Fiona held out her hand. Frederica gave her the megaphone. The Benbrook crew around them twittered in anticipation. Bri guessed they didn't get to see the big boss very often.

"I wanted to come here to thank all of you in person for performing a downright miracle in the time you were given," Fiona said. "Finish up your jobs by six o'clock tonight because we're hosting a party in the town to celebrate this new chapter in Marquardt's history."

Everyone cheered and tapped their glasses and cups with forks and spoons.

"I'll see you there." Fiona handed the megaphone to Frederica.

"Okay," Frederica said. "Eat up and get to work."

Everyone laughed and cheered.

Fiona looked at the travelers' table and gave a nod to Zen and then a slight cock of her head. Zen sighed but gave a slight nod back.

Fiona and Frederica went to an empty table near the window, followed by a pair of Benbrook staff, who walked to the second buffet table on the other side room after receiving instructions.

"Fiona wants to have a word," Zen said. She picked up her cup of tea. "Wish me luck."

Zen

ZEN PUT HER cup on the table, pulled out a chair, and sat across from Fiona and adjacent to Frederica, who was facing the dining room. Her aunts were casually stirring their tea and giving Zen the nonchalant treatment as their assistants put plates of food in front of them. Zen knew they were doing joyous flips and cartwheels on the inside.

"So, anything interesting going on?" Zen asked and took a sip of tea.

Fiona sighed and picked up a bag from the floor and put it on the table. "We got you something."

Zen frowned as she pulled the bag to her side of the table. She took out a folded T-shirt. She unfolded it and a tiny box fell to the table. She flashed a puzzled look as she picked up the plain box and lifted the lid. A pair of rings, nestled in cotton, sparkled back at her.

She looked up. "What's this?"

"That's the newly minted Welcome to Marquardt T-shirt. And those"—Fiona nodded at the box—"are our mother's rings. Much to her dismay, Frederica and I never bothered to tie the knot and you and Karma are the closest we'll ever get to having daughters. Karma is carrying on the family tradition of not being interested in getting married."

Zen sighed. "You've talked to her."

"She thought you might be able to put these rings to good use," Frederica said.

Zen stared at the rings. Last time she had seen them had been on her grandmother's aged hand. Could she really get so lucky to marry Bri? "Maybe."

"We won't embarrass you to introduce her to us now." Frederica gazed at the travelers' table. "But we expect to meet her at the party tonight."

Zen nodded. "It's a deal."

"Now go and enjoy your last day here," Fiona said.

Zen grinned. "We're going to the Roman ruins."

Frederica ruffled Zen's hair. "Have fun and good luck with your"—she nodded at the travelers' table—"side project."

Bri

BRI PULLED THE tiny van off the questionable lane onto little more than a couple of ruts and tried to control the bouncing up and down as much as possible. Joe's driving in the van ahead of them wasn't much better.

"Frederica said they'll be improving the lane back there," Zen said, as she grabbed the bar above her as the van rocked. "Put the parking lot there and make this a nice walking path."

"Excellent plan," Jon said from the back seat.

The other van disappeared around a small hill.

"Oh my God!" came Joe's voice from up ahead.

Bri exchanged looks with Zen, and they sputtered a laugh.

"I think they found the ruins," Zen said.

Bri rounded the hill and stopped the van before she crashed it. Stretched before them were seemingly acres and acres of crumbling ancient walls and towers and what looked like an amphitheater dug into a hillside.

"Wow," Kristy said.

Bri snapped out of it and pulled the van next to Joe's. The others were already wandering around talking to and aiming their cameras everywhere.

"Thanks for the lift," Jon said as he and Kristy hopped out of the van and strode between two crumbling walls that might have been where a gate had been.

Who could have guessed there were ruins of a Roman outpost in a meadow in Marquardt? Apparently, no one until a goat herder thirty years earlier had found remnants of a wall edging a stream after a heavy rain. Fortunately, a couple of archeologists, who had received their degrees at Cambridge before Marquardt had been cut off from the world, were wasting their knowledge working boring jobs in the old Marquardt regime. They convinced the dictator that Roman ruins looked really good to the rest of the world and were given permission to dig. Thirty years of digging uncovered an impressive pile of ruins.

Bri slipped out of her seat and pulled her camera from her backpack. Zen walked around the van to her.

"It's much bigger than I had imagined," Zen said.

Bri looked up at her. Eerie how Zen seemed to be able to read her mind. She really didn't think she could walk around all these ruins. Another thing to feel inadequate about amongst her solo traveling peers.

Zen turned around, as if studying the area. "I have an idea."

Bri gave her a wary look. "I never know whether to trust your ideas or not."

Zen laughed. "Okay, I'll give you a choice."

Bri let her wary look linger a few more seconds and then nodded. "Okay."

"You can either traipse around all the ruins or . . ." Zen turned to the hill they had just driven around.

Bri looked up the hill and then out at the acres of ruins and then back up the hill. "Option B." She gave Zen a side look. "You're pretty good at finding unique angles."

Zen glanced up and down at Bri. "I like to think I have a bit of a knack at it."

Bri shook her head, exasperated, but she couldn't help but be flattered by the idea that Zen found her attractive.

"Let's walk around the hill a bit so the others can't see what we're up to." Zen led the way on a narrow path that skirted the hill. "Looks like we're not the first ones who had this idea."

Bri started up a path etched out of the cropped grass that meandered up the small hill with Zen walking beside her at what Bri imagined was a snail's pace for Zen. But Zen seemed to be content sauntering next to her.

"Since we're getting to know each other," Bri said. "Does that mean I get to ask you questions that no one else knows the answer to?"

Zen cocked her head. "Sure. As long as I can ask you the same."

Bri bit her lip but realized she didn't have anything to hide. Well, Zen already seemed to know what she was not exactly hiding. "Okay."

Zen grinned as they topped the hill and walked toward several new-looking wooden benches facing the expanse of ruins. A sure sign of a Benbrook makeover.

"So"—Bri gave Zen a sidelong look—"where do you call home?"

Zen flashed amusement back at her. "I live over my sister's garage."

Bri squinted at her. "I admit, I wasn't expecting that answer. Where's your sister's house."

"Urbana. On one of those beautiful tree-lined streets just off campus."

Bri stopped walking. Zen turned to her.

"You know I went to Illinois," Bri said.

"Yes." Zen shrugged. "Small world."

Bri narrowed her eyes. "Why did your sister decide to settle in Urbana of all places?"

"She went to Illinois, too." Zen walked around a bench and sat on it.

"Really?" Bri frowned. "When?"

"Well"—Zen rubbed her chin—"she's a couple of years older than me . . ."

Bri frowned even more. "What did she major in?"

Zen leaned back and stretched out her legs. "Media and Cinema Studies."

Bri gazed at her for several moments and then sank down on the bench. "Down the hall from the Department of Journalism. You'd think I'd remember someone named Karma Benbrook."

"She decided to use our mother's name," Zen said. "I did, too, when I went to Berkeley."

"Which was?"

Zen cocked her head. "Petrelis."

Bri stared at the ruins that seemed to go on forever. *Oh my god.* "Your sister is Kay Pretrelis? She . . . she . . ."

Zen nodded. "Yes."

Bri put her hands over her face as she tried to piece together this unexpected collision of her past with now. Kay Pretrelis had stopped what could have been a very dangerous situation when a pair of drunk Frat boys tried to insinuate themselves on Bri and her date in a noisy crowded bar. The boys were not taking no for an answer and were getting belligerent about it.

Kay Pretrelis, who was as tall as her aunts and a well-known presence in the College of Media, walked up behind the boys and wrapped an arm around each of their necks.

"You boys want to go head-to-head with a black belt in Brazilian jiu-jitsu?" she asked in a calm, steady voice.

Their eyes bugged out as they tried to pull at her hold on them.

"I'm sorry, I didn't hear your answer." Kay rolled her eyes at Bri and her date, who were staring at her in awe.

"N-n-n-no," the frat boys pushed out between choking coughs.

"Also, when a woman says no. She means it." She pushed on her elbows a bit and the boys' eyes widened even more. "Got it?"

The boys tried nodding and saying yes.

"I don't believe you."

Kay let the boys struggle with tears running down their cheeks and croaking their promises for a couple of minutes, then let them go.

They coughed and fingered their throats and turned belligerent eyes to Kay.

"You'd better watch your back," one of them rasped.

Kay threw her head back and laughed. "You'd better get home to your mommies so they can wipe away your tears."

The boys straightened, indignant, and walked away, trying to act tough, but were too drunk to look like anything but pathetic, weak Frat boys.

Bri and her date couldn't thank Kay enough, but she just shrugged it off and told them about a bar where they wouldn't be bothered by the likes of drunken Frat boys.

"It was one of the first real dates I'd been on with a woman," Bri said. "So naïve back then."

"A few days later," Zen said, "those Frat boys and a bunch of their friends found Karma and her friends practicing jiu-jitsu in the rec center."

Bri turned to her. "Really?"

Zen grinned. "Yep. Let's just say, she knocked the swagger out of them in the most humiliating way possible in front of their friends. Better yet, being a cinema major, Karma liked to film her practices."

"Oh my god, it's on video?"

"Yep." Zen leaned forward with her elbows on her legs. "She sent a copy of it to them, saying she was making a documentary on Brazilian jiu-jitsu, and this was the perfect footage to demonstrate dealing with ordinary males who thought they could beat a female black belt. She said she'd leave the footage out if they behaved themselves around women."

"So, Karma really lives up to her name."

Zen laughed. A wonderful, free kind of laugh that seemed to come from a place of real joy. "Yeah, she really does."

"Just like you live up to your name," Bri said. "Which brings me to another question. Why do you and Karma have American accents?"

"That's an easy one," Zen said. "We have an American mother and yes, our father is British, but they decided to send us to American schools."

"Why were you born in Greece?"

"My father was working in a resort in Croatia, so my mother went to stay with her aunt and uncle further down the coast in Parga, Greece. Her mother was there to help with the birth. Parga is a tourist town, and my mother's family is also in the tourism business." Zen leaned back and gazed up at the sky. "Karma was born in India because my parents were beginning their exploration of eastern philosophies."

Bri frowned. "Does your father still work for the business?"

Zen shook her head. "They decided to create a Buddhist meditation retreat in California when Karma and I were in high school."

"Your father doesn't seem to be like his sisters," Bri said.

Zen barked a laugh. "He's lucky to have them because he would have been very unhappy running a multi-billion-dollar empire. Fortunately, Fiona and Frederica thrive on it."

Bri was dying to ask what it was like to be so rich that Zen could do or buy anything she wanted and not think twice about it. On the other hand, it was refreshing to see that she didn't. That her home was over a garage attached to an old house in a university faculty neighborhood.

"So, when did you make the connection between me and the girl Kay saved in college?"

Zen turned to her with a sheepish expression. "Well, when you were doing features for that TV station, Karma showed me an article about you in the alumni magazine and told me you were the one she had rescued back in college."

"And you recognized me when you saw my vlog," Bri said.

"Yeah." Zen gazed at her. "I was happy to see you were able to pivot after getting laid off."

"My crew on the features, Sarah and Josh, and I decided to take what we knew and make our own show," Bri said. "Control our own destiny."

"And it worked. You have almost three million followers." Zen gave her head a shake. "More than any solo traveler."

Bri sat up. "Present company excepted."

"Huh?"

"Present company excepted." Bri frowned at Zen's baffled expression.

"You mean my Instagram?" Zen asked. "It's only nine-hundred-thousand and something."

Bri squinted at her. Why was she being so obtuse? "Your YouTube channel."

Zen, still looking baffled, nodded. "Karma runs the vlog. I looked at it when I first started, but I just couldn't watch myself, so I put it completely into her hands."

Bri could only stare at Zen. "Surely, she gives you reports on how many followers you have so you know how the channel's doing."

Zen stared out at the ruins. "When I quit my job, I didn't have any idea what to do with my life. I moved into the apartment above Karma's garage and spent my days wandering around campus and both Urbana and Champaign. Then one beautiful fall day, I walked to Rantoul and back. After that I was walking all over the place."

"You discovered a hidden skill?"

Zen chuckled. "Yeah, something like that. Anyway, I realized walking was a unique way of seeing the world. At about the same time, regular people taking off and traveling all over the place was becoming popular on YouTube. So, Karma and I sat out on the front porch one evening tossing around the idea of a walking travel channel and working out the logistics of it."

"That's kind of what Sarah, Josh, and I did after we got laid off," Bri said.

Zen nodded. "We set parameters for the channel. After we worked out all the stuff we needed, we came up with a plan to finance the first year, then after that the channel would run off of what we made from YouTube. If it didn't make enough, we'd shut it down." Zen held out her hands. "I've been walking ever since, so I figured it was making enough money to cover all the expenses. It helps that I try to stay at Benbrook properties or with friends, not to mention use the transportation perks from being a Benbrook, to even out the ups and downs of viewers per vlog."

All of Bri's certainties shattered in her shocked mind. "You really don't know how many subscribers you have?"

Zen shook her head. "No idea. I figured it was about what I have on Instagram."

"You don't know that you have four-point-six million subscribers?" Bri asked.

Zen stared at her, shocked. Too late, Bri realized she might have exploded something in Zen's contented insular world.

"I, uh . . ." Zen took a deep breath. "I had no idea."

"People think we're archrivals in the solo travel world."

"What?"

"All they see are the numbers."

Zen gave her head a shake. "Well, I guess those numbers mean I can keep walking." She took a deep breath. "Sorry. I really had no idea. I thought you were the queen of solo travel." She flashed a sheepish look.

"I was afraid I . . . I don't know, burst a bubble or something."

Zen turned her body to Bri and took both her hands. "Just a shock. I'm more surprised over the archrival thing. Biggest fan with a massive crush. Yes."

As Bri gazed at Zen who watched her with sincere, affectionate eyes, she saw just another person trying to figure out the world like everyone else. Zen hadn't gone to live in a mansion or penthouse apartment or on a yacht when she quit her job. She hadn't become a jetsetter or a rich person throwing her money around. She went to live in a college town in a quaint old house in a neighborhood filled with students and faculty.

The supposed rivalry for subscribers wasn't what made a part of her hesitant about pursuing some kind of relationship with Zen. Was she afraid of not being able to fit into Zen's world?

"You know, you're making it extremely difficult not to kiss you," Zen whispered. "But you never know who's watching."

Bri reluctantly pulled her hands from Zen's and faced the ruins. "Maybe we should get some footage before everyone else discovers this spot."

Bri

"BEFORE WE GO out and celebrate," Bri said as she stared out the window in their hotel room. "I want to make a vlog, like the one you did before this trip, directly to my followers."

"Okay." Zen sounded puzzled.

Bri half-turned to Zen. "You said there was a nice view from the roof?"

"Yes. Frederica's been working on turning the roof into a beer garden," Zen said.

Bri nodded, fighting her reluctance to step out of character so to speak. But she knew she had to do it. A first hint that her channel might have some changes, that she might have some changes . . . She glanced at Zen.

"Okay. Let's do this." She went to her desk. "Do you mind being my camera person?"

Zen grinned. "It would be my great pleasure."

Bri shook her head. Would she ever get used to the idea that Zen Benbrook really really *really* liked her?

She picked up her camera and microphone. "Is this all I need?"

"Yep," Zen said. "The sun should be perfect if you want the village and the mountains in the background."

"That would be great." Bri took a deep breath as they stepped into the hall.

"If it helps," Zen said, "I was hesitant to do my pre-trip vlog."

Bri turned to her. "Really?"

Zen shrugged as they approached the elevators. "Seven years is a long time to be doing things one way. A part of me felt like I was betraying a pact I had made with my subscribers." She chuckled. "The more logical part knew I was overthinking it. And I was."

"I know I don't have to do this," Bri said. "But I feel like I need to."

They stepped onto the elevator.

"Whether we want to or not, we feel like we have some kind of obligation to our viewers." Zen pressed the button to the fifth floor. "Maybe they like something different every once in a while."

Bri sighed as she watched each floor number light up.

"Have you lost viewers or subscribers during this week?"

Bri turned to Zen. "Sarah has reported an increase in viewership and a spike in new followers. But it's because of Marquardt. Not because I'm with a group and doing things that I normally wouldn't do on my vlogs."

The elevator bell sounded, and the door slid open. They stepped into a scene that looked like a tornado had whipped through and was now eerily silent.

Zen led the way to the stairwell. "Frederica will have this floor cleared and cleaned before the first paying guests arrive."

"What does she do when she's not leading the cavalry?" Bri asked as they walked up two short flights of stairs.

Zen pushed open the door at the top of the steps, and Bri shaded her eyes against the intense evening sun.

"She's the COO of Benbrook International." Zen walked to a corner of the middle part of roof where the two wings met. Long rustic benches and tables and an equally rustic-looking bar on one side filled the space. Waist-high log walls ran along the edges of the roof. She looked around and nodded. "When it's open, they'll put up umbrellas and banners and lights and other festive stuff. It'll also be a good space for private parties."

Bri walked to the edge of the roof and gazed down at the town. The milling people made the road look like a living organism with the long tables of food and drink—courtesy of Benbrook—snaking against the buildings. The sinking sun illuminated the white of the buildings and bathed the valley in that magical orange glow before sunset. She raised the camera and captured the moment and bubbled over with the idea that she was not only seeing it but feeling it. Feeling the beauty. Feeling the magic. Breathing in the aroma of cooking food floating on the breeze and the hum of thousands of people finally embracing the fact that they were truly free from tyranny.

As darkness infiltrated the town, the light from streetlights and shops and hanging lanterns and strings of fairy lights turned the scene into glowing ambers and yellows, transcending the magic to something she'd never experienced before.

She finally remembered to breathe and switched off her camera. She looked around for Zen, who was sitting at the end of a bench in the dying light, flying a drone.

Zen looked up, smiled, and brought in her drone. "Ready?"

"Yeah." She really was ready. "Where should I stand?"

Zen took Bri's camera and guided her to a spot that captured the last of the sun and the lights rising from below and from the Alps beyond. She squeezed Bri's hand. "You'll do great."

Bri took a deep breath and nodded.

Zen positioned herself so she could capture Bri and the festive backdrop. "Ready when you are."

Bri relaxed her body and caught Zen's gentle, encouraging grin. Yeah. She could think of worse changes in her life. She nodded. "Ready."

Zen pressed the record button, and Bri gazed at the lens. "When I began this adventure, I never imagined I'd be attending a street party celebrating a new Marquardt excited about welcoming visitors. Eight of us came as solo travelers and are leaving as comrades. We're even discussing doing some more adventures together. I admit I was a little wary about being a part of a group after going solo for so many years, but it turned out to be a pleasant change." She flicked her eyes to Zen. "I couldn't help but notice the discussions on how I seemed to spend a lot of time with Zen Traveler." She chuckled. "Some of you have pretty amazing imaginations. So, I'll just say, we've all just been playing it by ear. No, we weren't put together in the same room for potential drama. It was Marquardtian practicality to room us females by age. And you do know that the drama comes from all of you. Zen and I have never considered each other rivals, much less archrivals. In fact, she's holding the camera for me right now. Wave to the nice people, Zen."

Zen, looking amused, waved her hand in front of the lens.

"I don't think I would have made it through this week without Zen showing me how to just relax and not to worry about my vlogs being so different from what you're used to from me. I came to realize I might have been in a bit of a rut and mixing things up a little hasn't been such a bad thing. A surprising number of you have enjoyed watching my interactions with Zen, which is good because we've enjoyed our little adventures together. So"—Bri glanced at Zen and then smiled at the lens—"don't be surprised if we get together for more adventures. But that's something to think about in the future. Right now, we have a celebration to attend and then, as I mentioned before this trip, I'm taking a few weeks off from travel, then will be back with a series exploring the Greek Isles. So, enjoy the Marquardt party with me and I'll see you in Greece."

Bri held her position for several seconds and then relaxed. Zen stopped recording.

"One take." Zen approached Bri and held the camera out to her. "I'm impressed."

"My tv background does come in handy." Bri took the camera.

Zen stuffed her hands into her pockets and stared out at the town. "So, you think you might want to do more adventures with me?"

Bri gazed at Zen. Her hesitant shyness was not only endearing but darn near irresistible. She mentally shook her head. Face it. Everything about Zen was irresistible. Why was she so hesitant about letting go and giving in to her feelings?

She returned her gaze to the town. "Maybe."

Zen slid closer to Bri until their shoulders touched. She teased Bri's fingers with her fingers until they were intertwined.

Bri struggled against the onslaught of sweetness.

"Think of the adventures we could have," Zen said in a soft voice. "On camera . . . and off."

Bri almost stopped breathing . "You're not making it easy."

Zen leaned in and Bri shivered from her wispy breath on her ear. "Good. Gives me hope." She stepped back and gave Bri's hand a gentle tug. "Time to experience a Marquardt street party, compliments of my over-achieving family."

11
Day 7
Zen

ZEN TRIED NOT to gaze at Bri who sat in the seat across from her in the back of the small van, thankfully driven by a Benbrook staffer. Bri was looking out the window and glancing at Zen every few minutes. Zen knew what she was asking of Bri was way out of her tidy, controlled world, unlike the world Zen had grown up in, where change and spontaneity were a part of everyday life.

While she was raised to never flaunt their wealth, she also grew up not having to consider the cost of spontaneity. The knowledge of this privilege had made her even more low key about being rich. The only thing she had ever set a budget for was the walking vlog, and it was making enough money for her to be spontaneous without worrying about cost.

She shook her head at the irony as she glanced at Bri, who was watching something out the window.

"Wow." Mick half stood in his seat as he pointed out the window. "They really did a good job of fixing up the border."

Zen joined the others in aiming their cameras out the windows. The cold war bunker buildings had been painted white with timber frames and now had a big bright welcome sign and information center. The guards and gate were gone. Marquardt was officially open.

Bri put down her camera and turned to Zen, grinning. Zen returned her grin as the other travelers chattered to each other and to their cameras.

Zen's phone vibrated. She pulled it from her pocket. A text from Karma.

"I've gotten word that walkers have entered Marquardt from Italy. They posted a video of them doing a dance on the border and making a grand proclamation that Marquardt is henceforth open."

Zen laughed. She loved her crazy Zenites.

Bri gave her a curious look.

"Walkers have already infiltrated Marquardt from Italy," Zen said.

"Did you say walkers are in Marquardt?" Mick asked.

Everyone cheered.

"I guess our work here is done," Sally said.

"Know any more countries that need the tourist-ready test?" Joe asked. "It was fun being a part of history instead of just tromping around it."

They chattered on as Zen and Bri gazed at each other. Were they trying to capture the last few moments of this experience together and part as friends or . . .

The van started up a steep climb and then made a sharp turn past the outer buildings of the village. In a few minutes, the van pulled over across from the train station.

This was it. Zen tried not to look at Bri as she gathered her stuff and let her go first into the aisle. She followed Bri off the bus and didn't quite know what to do. The others had gathered in front of the train station. It turned out they were all headed south into Italy and decided to keep the party going a little longer and take the same train.

Bri pulled her case to the middle of the road. She took out the main camera from her bag and put it in an easy to reach side pocket. She affixed her GoPro to the strap on her backpack and the second one to the ribbon on her fedora.

The travelers were watching her with curious fascination.

Zen frowned, trying to figure out what she was doing.

Bri finished setting up her cameras and turned to Zen. "Eight miles aren't going to get walked by themselves."

Zen could only stare at her. She never even considered that Bri would choose to walk to the villa.

Sally put her hands on her hips. "For Pete's sake. Do we have to draw you a map?"

"What are you waiting for?" Mick yelled.

The travelers' yelled encouragements that coalesced into a chant of "Go, go, go."

Zen gave her head a shake and walked to Bri. "I can call a car."

"I know." Bri adjusted her backpack, hit record on the GoPro on the backpack strap, and strode down the road toward the valley.

Zen glanced at the travelers, who were grinning and collapsing into each other in silly laughter . . . Jon slapped a few Euros into Sally's hand.

Zen jogged after Bri and fell into step beside her. Bri flashed a smile at her, and Zen stumbled a bit.

"I won't be able to carry you," Bri said without breaking her stride.

Zen laughed as she pulled out her drone and released it in front of them to capture the moment her heart was at last whole and belonged to the woman of her dreams.

Bri

BRI SAT AGAINST a pile of pillows and stared into the dusky room at the arched multi-paned window that had a view of the mountains in the daytime. The room was open and airy with delicate Louis XIV furniture, tastefully ornate with almost understated elegance. She pulled the sheets up around her as the chilly air gave her goosebumps. She had to admit they were the softest sheets she'd ever felt. The bed wasn't too shabby either. She chuckled. Everything down to the cloud-soft towels and the delicate soap dish that was a work of art, probably cost more than anything she owned.

This was Zen's world. She gazed down at Zen sprawled under the covers and resisted tousling the curls on her forehead, not wanting to wake her.

Much to Bri's surprise, she didn't feel intimidated by the ritzy surroundings. It helped that dinner was shared with the locals enjoying one last free meal before the Villa opened to paying visitors tomorrow. The joyous, carefree atmosphere was anything but stodgy. It also helped to learn that ordinary Zen and rich Zen were truly the same person.

"Too far away," Zen mumbled.

Bri smiled as she looked at Zen who still had her eyes closed. She scooted down into the warm nest of the bed and faced Zen, who watched her through sleepy half-closed eyes. Bri finally found something that Zen could do to exhaustion. *Lucky me.*

Bri felt Zen's hand on hers.

"Marry me," Zen mumbled.

Bri rolled her eyes. "You're as bad as those U-Haul lesbians."

"Engaged?"

"Go back to sleep." Bri couldn't stop her grin.

"Go steady?" Zen breathed, her lids drifting over her eyes.

Bri shook with laughter. She couldn't think of anything she wanted to do more than go steady. Yeah. Going steady could be fun.

T. J. Mindancer may be a figment of someone's imagination or just someone who likes to imagine she's a figment while she creates worlds for her characters to inhabit. She has spent her life working with books as an academic librarian and as an editor for two publishing companies and has had some of her scribbled words published under a couple of pen names—at least one, not a figment. Her work includes the Tales of Emoria series of books and shorter tales set in the Emoria world.